I0685803

SCORING REAGAN

A NOVEL

THE PANTHER PLAYER SERIES

FBI Anti-Piracy Warning: The unauthorized reproduction or distribution of a copyrighted work is illegal. Criminal copyright infringement, including infringement without monetary gain, is investigated by the FBI and is punishable by up to five years in federal prison and a fine of $250,000.

Scoring Reagan
First Edition

Copyright © 2020 Tori Kron
All rights reserved. Printed in the United States of America. For information, address Acorn Publishing, LLC, 3943 Irvine Blvd. Ste. 218, Irvine, CA 92602.

No part of this book may be used or reproduced in any manner whatsoever, including Internet usage, without written permission from the author.

This story is a work of fiction. References to real people, events, establishments, organizations, or locales are intended only to provide a sense of authenticity and are used fictitiously. All other characters, and all incidents and dialogue are drawn from the author's imagination and are not to be construed as real.

Acorn Editor: Holly Kammier

Cover design by ebooklaunch.com

Book interior formatted by Debra Cranfield Kennedy

ISBN—Paperback 978-1-947392-76-2

For Kyle and all the brothers who kept their cool
when a friend started dating their little sister.

Chapter One

"**I** STILL can't believe you flew all the way to Atlanta just to be my date tonight."

Reagan Cassidy's starry gaze flashed to her companion. Positioned on the other side of the elevator was the one and only Deacon Bailey.

With his light brown skin, height for days, and brawny muscles, the Panthers basketball star had been the perfect tool to exact revenge on her cheater, pilot ex.

"You put up with my whining after my shoulder surgery last year, so I owed you, at least, this," he replied.

"Probably more," Reagan said, remembering his newborn like neediness.

"Probably."

A gleam shone in the starting guard's mahogany eyes. Like textured wood grain, the light and dark rings of his irises contrasted youth and wisdom.

Wisdom, Reagan reminded herself while looping an auburn lock behind her ear, would tell her not to stare too intently at any one of Deacon's splendid features. After all, as her brother's best friend, he was off limits.

Despite the fact that she'd had a crush on him for years, Deacon was out of reach.

Metaphorically speaking, of course.

Throughout the party, he'd stayed glued to Reagan's side. Placing his hand upon her hip as they danced. His muscled body swaying in rhythm with hers.

But that had been the point. To deceive everyone into believing they were a couple when they weren't.

Yet, nothing about her laughter or the overwhelming buzz that hummed through her five, nine frame had felt fake.

Suddenly heated, Reagan's back leaned into the wood paneled interior, her palm floating to the front of her cotton dress.

Deacon's thick brows knitted with concern as her body twisted with discomfort. "Are you okay?"

"I'm fine. Just tired." Reagan attempted a thin smile to reinforce the claim.

But she wasn't fine.

She was yearning for her brother's best friend.

A finely formed athlete who was handsome as sin.

And standing next to her in a *very* small elevator.

In a hotel.

Alone.

Because temptation couldn't knock on the door and leave without causing a scene. An unrelenting presence, it had to hold in the doorbell, ringing over and over for all to hear.

Not buying her half-hearted declaration, Deacon, always the protector, freed his hands from his khakis and moved a bit closer. However, the athlete's helpful intent only added to Reagan's agitation.

In an attempt to escape the athlete's close proximity, Reagan side stepped to the right, but her shoulder met the thick wall after a two inch slide.

"You didn't have to ride up with me, you know? I could have made it to my room by myself," Reagan said.

"I'm on the seventh floor, so you're on the way." Deacon rocked back and forth on his dress shoes. "Besides, Miller would want me to see you back safe."

That's right. *Miller*.

Her brother.

Deacon's best friend.

Reagan focused on the term. Friend. That's what she and Deacon were.

Friends.

Dinging their arrival, metal doors pulled apart to reveal the small lobby adjacent from Reagan's room. She heaved a sigh of relief and swore she heard her escort do the same.

But why? Had their evening together been that unpleasant for him?

He seemed like he'd enjoyed himself while spinning about the dance floor, but maybe alcohol had her reading the signals wrong? Or maybe the make shift paparazzi her co-workers had transformed into dampened his fun?

"I'm sorry if tonight was too much," Reagan said. "With everyone snapping pictures and such."

"I didn't love the extra attention, but I can't fault them for being excited."

Reagan could sense the warmth of the athlete's arm as it hovered around her back and across to her waist, ushering her out of the elevator.

Deacon's lack of contact came as no surprise seeing as he was the epitome of a perfect gentleman. Outside of a basketball court, he never pushed boundaries. Never even came within a foot of crossing them. Because Deacon was a good man and a good friend to all.

Especially Miller.

Which was why she was crazy to even dare to think of Deacon as anything else.

"I'm good from here," Reagan said, motioning to the nearby line of doors.

Ready to escape the small confines of their transport, Reagan trod two hasty steps, but her sluggish toe caught on the gap between the lift and the wood planks. A shriek escaped her lips as she tumbled forward. Grappling to steady her stance, Reagan latched her red nails into Deacon's muscular arm.

Used to quick movement, the athlete wasn't caught completely off guard, but his strained face showed he wasn't prepared to support her full body weight.

Deacon clasped Reagan's waist and pulled her into his midsection with a swift thrust. She still couldn't secure her footing, so the momentum of the pull worked against him, spun them in a circle, and sent their twisted bodies crashing to the carpeted floor. A protective hand cupped Reagan's head, shielding her from a damaging blow. But Deacon's rock hard body pressed against hers, stealing her breath with his weight.

Eyes flickering with lust, Deacon held her gaze.

With barely an inch separating their lips, electricity vibrated between them, sparking through her veins, and sending a laborious heartbeat pulsing in her ear.

Reagan's body lit with fire as she pushed her palms against the athlete's firm chest. She had to get out from under him before she caved to the temptation of staying put.

"You're crushing me."

"I'm sorry." Deacon scrambled to his feet and held out a helping hand. "Are you okay?"

"I'm fine," she said, hoping the athlete couldn't read her body language which had to be screaming anything but.

Ignoring Deacon's open palm, Reagan lifted to her wedges, fiddling in her clutch to find her room key. Trembling fingers weren't made for a solid grip, so the blue plastic floated to the ground.

"I've got it," Reagan and Deacon echoed at the same time, simultaneously dipping for the card.

Reaching out, their fingers swept in a spellbinding brush. Frozen by the touch, their eyes locked long enough for Reagan to decipher a gloss of longing coating Deacon's dark pupils.

She pulled away as Deacon's hand wrapped the key, but they held the intense stare as they found an upright position.

Palm opening, Deacon raised the plastic card to Reagan.

Fingers brushing against his callused hand, searing heat rushed over her pale skin like the first warm crackle from a freshly lit fire. Flames of equal intensity flashed within Deacon's dark eyes.

Like a moth drawn to light, Reagan's body shifted forward until she could feel the warmth of Deacon's breath hot on her lips. She studied the tug of war between reason and want pulling in his eyes, feeling the same struggle in her heart.

They could have tonight.

A brief affair.

No one else would have to know.

But the sun would rise on tomorrow. And what then?

Would everything be different? Could their friendship ever be the same?

Did she want it to be the same? Could she settle for being Deacon's friend while feeling the inferno blazing inside of her chest?

Reagan's lips parted to speak her concern, but Deacon silenced her as a strangled rumble sounded from his throat.

His warm mouth crashed into hers, stealing her breath and thoughts as his hands pulled her close. She opened to him, no longer caring for the consequence of what they were doing. Reagan was swept up in his lips, caressing, pulling, wanting all that he had to give.

Reagan wrapped her fingers around Deacon's stout bicep for

stability as he pushed her taut body backwards. A shiver shot down her spine when his hips pinned hers tight against the lobby wall. Heat spread up the curve of her chest and to the back of her neck as his plump lips thrust against hers. The athlete's tongue swirled with a fierceness Reagan had never felt, and fire seared down to her toes. She was certain the carpet would start smoking at any moment.

"This," Deacon began as he trailed kisses along her jaw, "cannot happen."

Reagan's hands curved over Deacon's sculpted chest. His body was as well defined as the ancient Greek sculptures displayed in the Met. Only he wasn't made of clay. No, this man was full of warm flesh, and Reagan wanted nothing more than to rip his shirt off and feel his hot skin on hers.

"I think we've passed that point," Reagan whispered, and Deacon moaned as the heat from her breath brushed his ear.

The athlete fisted her soft curls and pulled Reagan's lips in to his for another impassioned embrace. While her mouth melted into his, Reagan hastily undid two small buttons near the top of his shirt, dipping her fingers under the cotton to trace the slight curve of his collarbone.

"I—" Before he could respond, Deacon's phone vibrated in his pocket, pulling him from their trance.

"Whoever it is can wait." Reagan sucked the soft spot below his ear, hoping to draw him back into the reverie. But always responsible, Deacon lifted the phone from its nook and glanced at the glowing screen.

"Damn it." His flat palm slammed into the wall.

"What?"

Reagan's heart thumped against her chest, uncertain if Deacon was angry with himself or what he read on the display. Either way, the scowl on his face said it was bad. Her companion had gone from a hot coal to an ice cube in a matter of seconds.

"What is it?" she asked again.

"I'm sorry," Deacon muttered, pushing away. His eyes fluttered shut as if he needed the darkness to focus. "This was a mistake."

Too stunned to speak, Reagan's lashes fluttered with disbelief.

What had she done wrong?

She'd felt the intensity that radiated from his body to hers. It was unlike anything she'd ever known before.

How could something that electric be a mistake?

"I'm sorry," Deacon said, backing away. "Truly."

Still catching her breath, Reagan's body sank to the floor as she watched Deacon pace to the elevator. He climbed into the metal box without so much as another glance in her direction.

Ouch.

The young woman knew sparks could burn your skin, but the after effect of dancing in the flames stung more than she imagined.

Tears welling on her lower lids, Reagan's face met her palms. She knew better than this.

Men were always unreliable.

Always changing their minds.

Reagan learned long ago not to count on men, and she needed to remember that lesson.

WITHOUT LOOKING BACK, Deacon's brown loafers plowed into the elevator. Ensconced in all that is Reagan, he hadn't paid attention on the ride up, but he was relieved to find the lift with wooden walls instead of a modern, mirrored interior. The athlete could barely stand to be in his own skin, much less look at his stupid, smug face.

What the hell had he been thinking?

He hadn't been. That was the problem.

Not with his brain at least.

Until the call from Miller had knocked Deacon from his stupor.

From day one, Cassidy made it more than clear that his little sister was off limits to his teammates. With Reagan's flowing, red hair, long legs, and feisty personality, she'd always been a temptation, and plenty of the guys gave Miller shit by pretending like they were going to act on the enticement.

But no one actually did.

Not only did Miller's penchant for fighting deter the team, but the Panthers also knew that in order to play successfully they had to have trust. A team couldn't function well enough to win with discord between athletes. And no one wanted to be the cause of a losing streak. It was a surefire way to get involuntarily traded.

Deacon rapped his forehead against the wall, hoping to knock some sense back into place.

He'd managed to keep his attraction in check for years. Yet, after a single night alone with Reagan he'd been swept up in her storm, that dress, and the way those heels made her calves curve into her sumptuous thighs.

And her eyes. Stunning blue sapphires that sparkled like moonlight on the ocean. They hovered perfectly above her button nose and luscious mouth. Lips that caressed with a craving. Reagan's kiss was a hurricane of passion, but one he couldn't live again.

Not if he intended to keep his best friend and the team that had become his second family.

Aware the calm of the eye only lasted a moment before the whirling wind started to sweep a person up again, Deacon aimed to get away from Reagan before he spiraled out of control.

He had to leave the hotel.

Deacon's palms ran over his buzzed scalp. No, that wouldn't be enough distance. If he stayed in the same city, Deacon would be drawn back into Reagan's spell.

He had to hop a flight and leave Atlanta. Return to Indianapolis immediately. Where he'd be safe.

Deacon gulped. Until Reagan arrived.

As Miller's sister, there was no way he could avoid her forever. And now that he knew the strawberry flavor of her lips, he'd be tempted to taste them again.

A heavy breath flowed from deep within Deacon's chest.

He was royally screwed, and he hadn't even gotten laid.

Chapter Two

"**V**ICTORY beers on me." Deacon returned from the bar carrying two buckets brimming with brown bottles.

His broad shoulders wedged between Miller and his girlfriend Kate as he placed silver pails atop the lifted table at Lockerbie's Pub.

His towering friend's green eyes narrowed at the intrusion, but the twenty-seven-year-old smiled at the crowd gathered round and pretended not to notice Miller's contempt.

Still, the irony of the situation wasn't lost on Deacon.

Not long ago, his best friend wanted nothing more than to get away from Kate and her lackluster lifestyle. But under the influence of a red dress and few hard learned lessons, the Panther's most infamous player had gone from brawling bad boy to adoring boyfriend. Now, six months deep into a committed relationship, Miller couldn't keep his hands off her.

"We're not that bad, are we?" Miller's fingers ran through his sandy strands.

"Depends on the day," Deacon replied, tugging at the blue collar of his button up.

Not that Deacon could blame his friend. He'd recently discovered the intense spell a woman could cast on a man to make him act out of character.

Miller's light brow lifted. "Jealous?"

"You know I'm not," Deacon lied, his eyes scanning the crowded bar until they landed on Reagan, who was approaching the group.

Nearly nine months had passed since the night they'd let their inhibitions slide. The night they'd started something they couldn't seem to finish.

Literally.

He and Reagan had sworn to keep their distance more times than he could count, yet like a boomerang, they always circled back around to their problematic position.

And their trouble seemed to grow with time.

Every stage he and Reagan caved to their desire to be together, something went awry.

Like Miller landing behind bars.

Or Kate stumbling onto their secret.

The universe had sent them sign after sign to stay apart. Yet, they struggled to heed her warning.

"What I know is that you haven't even been on a date lately. Why is that?" Miller questioned.

"Alone time is spiritually cleansing," Deacon replied.

Only it wasn't.

His reality of wanting Reagan and not being able to have her was agonizing.

Not that Deacon could admit that to his friend without catastrophic consequences.

"With all the action you could get, this self-imposed monkhood is crazy." Miller took a swig from a clear, plastic cup.

Tugging the container from Miller's grip, Deacon sniffed the substance. It was odorless and lacked the sharp sting of liquor.

Apparently, he wasn't the only one who'd tumbled off the deep end for a woman.

"I'm crazy? You're drinking water at a bar. When did you even find out they serve that here?"

"I'm being more mindful these days." Miller's green eyes glanced toward Kate, the slender brunette, who was standing next to him chatting with the rookie.

Deacon shoved the cup back to his friend. "Yeah, but that doesn't mean you have to be lame. I mean, *water? You?*"

In a few short months, life as Deacon knew it had flipped. Miller had become a responsible adult, while Deacon had thrown inhibition to the wind, dancing on the boundary line of trouble with Reagan. And Deacon, always karma conscious, wasn't used to being bad.

"Who is drinking *agua* after a win?" Stella Davila's sharp voice cut into the players' conversation. The Panther's public relations guru wasn't known for softness, so her severe frown on her face was an attribute Deacon had grown accustomed to over the years.

"Miller," Deacon replied, palm patting his friend's back. "Apparently, he's responsible now."

"That would explain why I've had some free time lately," Stella smirked, pushing back her long, chestnut locks.

"Ha ha," Miller quipped. "I was not that bad."

"Either way, water doesn't work tonight. Grab a beer, Cassidy." The bombshell pointed to the half empty bucket of beers. "We're celebrating."

"You usually tell us to calm down. Now you want us to drink?" Deacon's forehead furrowed. "I swear, everyone has gone mad."

The spiritual athlete was more than aware that the pending spring equinox could affect moods and inspire behavioral changes, but spring fever was starting to take on a whole new meaning.

"I'm only condoning it because tonight is a special occasion." A sly sparkle twinkled in Stella's dark eyes. "I have news."

Following her own command, the hem of Stella's fuchsia dress lifted, as did her winter coat, as her arm stretched toward a bottle.

Spring air in the Midwestern metropolis didn't hold heat the way the native Puerto Rican was accustomed, so she often over dressed in seasonally inappropriate apparel. Not that anyone dared to call her out on it. Going to battle with Stella was setting oneself up for failure.

"News, huh?" Kate's bare arms leaned into the table top as she shifted her focus from the rookie to her friend. "This should be good."

"Please say it has nothing to do with me," Miller said, hovering over Kate's bent form. "I'm into my low key life right now."

"I much prefer this version of him, too," Reagan said, perching on a stool across the table.

Deacon sighed. Didn't they all? It was why he and Reagan were willing to forgo their own wants and desires to see him at peace.

"Agreed." A bemused smile formed on Stella's nude lips. "And thanks to Miller's streak of good behavior, for once, I'm able to focus on another player."

Deacon's pulse hastened as Stella's cutting gaze shifted his direction.

His brown eyes flashed to Reagan, whose temple was creased with concern.

Was this the end of their secret? And what was he going to say to Miller if Stella revealed their attempt at an affair? Sorry wasn't likely to cut it.

Then again, could it even be considered a romantic tryst since they'd only shared a second base stint in a hallway and a few chance encounters? All of which had been painfully interrupted.

Deacon shifted his weight from left to right. Terminology would probably be irrelevant to Miller considering the basic idea was the same.

He'd broken the cardinal rule of the bro code and fooled around with his best friend's sister.

"If not, Miller, then who?" Kate cut in as her nose wrinkled with confusion.

Stella tipped her bottle top in Deacon's direction, putting the athlete on center stage.

He loathed excessive attention on a regular day, but his was even worse. Deacon wanted Stella to point her heated gaze at absolutely anyone else.

Showing she was also leery of her friend's intentions, Kate's soprano voice pitched higher. "Why? I mean, Deacon hasn't done anything to draw attention to himself lately."

The young woman knew her statement was false, yet she said the words with stunning believability.

Stella brushed her long, inky hair behind her shoulders as her eyes lit with a knowing glow. "I think we all know that's not true."

Catching Kate's anxious fingers rap against the dark wood, Deacon shot the tall woman a reassuring smile, but her thin lips were tight with tension as her blue eyes darted between him and Reagan.

What did she have to be nervous about?

Unless, she already knew what Stella was going to share.

The two were best friends, after all. It was a well-known fact that they had a weekly date for tacos and margaritas. And tequila didn't have a reputation for inhibiting conversation.

Deacon's dark pupils glanced Reagan's way to see how she was holding up under the building pressure.

When their gazes met, her plump lips forced a smile that did little to boost the athlete's comfort level. And her apparel only added to his state of agitation.

Sporting skintight, dark denim that hugged her small hips, and a Panther's vee neck tee sculpted to her perky chest, Deacon was having a hard time not starring. Especially when her fingers tousled the auburn waves that framed her face.

The starting guard couldn't help but think about the way those silky curls wound through his hands. The way her thick lashes lowered when he brushed a kiss to her pink lips. The way she sighed at his gentle touch. It was movie worthy magic.

An elbow from Kate's direction jammed into Deacon's side, warning the athlete to redirect his attention.

Maybe she hadn't revealed their secret after all? Or was she simply alerting him to be on guard?

"Enough with the suspense," Miller clamored over the blaring juke box. "Tell us your big news, Stella. What's all the fuss about?"

"A budding relationship." The knee length hem of Stella's dress swayed as her stilettos strutted toward Deacon.

"Oh, no," Kate gasped. As if she anticipated Miller taking a swing, her thin fingers clutched his arm.

Deacon felt the tension rising in his throat while he watched the white in Reagan's eyes double.

"It can't be Deac." Miller's arm fell from his girlfriend's shoulder and shifted to pat his friends back. "He's not seeing anyone, and he hates blind dates."

Heat rushed to Deacon's face, but his light brown skin didn't easily give away his flustered state. However, Reagan's porcelain complexion fired red, as if she might burst into flames at any moment.

"Well, there's no easy way to say this, then." Stella paused to let anticipation build as she leaned into the table top.

Deacon's eyes scrunched as he prepped for Miller's punch to pound his jaw. Or his abdomen. The athlete wasn't sure which route his friend would choose.

Regardless, Deacon wasn't going to try to block the furious blow. By conspiring with Reagan, he'd broken Miller's honor code of male friendship, so his deception deserved the strike.

A hundred even.

Possibly more.

Stella cleared her throat and waited for the crowd to refocus their wandering attention before speaking again. Clapping her hands together to secure every last ear, she proclaimed, "Deacon better learn to like setups because he was just selected as this year's celebrity bachelor for the Single In The City series."

Kate's jaw dropped as Miller and the other Panther players whooped with excitement. Claps echoed throughout the small interior.

"What?" Deacon spouted over the uproar. His body flooded with relief at not being exposed for a traitor, just to be overtaken by a new pounding in his chest. "You signed me up for that stupid dating game show?"

"*Actually*, you did so well hosting the Donor Foundation's telethon last fall, the organizers came to me. They thought you'd be the perfect candidate, and I agree." Stella's smile lifted.

"But I hate speaking in front of people," Deacon protested. "The telethon was a fluke. And there were prompt cards to read. I can't handle being the subject of a legitimate show."

"The series will only be broadcast online, mostly in the Indy area, so it's not like I'm throwing you onto national primetime." Stella waved off the athlete's concern. "Besides, it's great publicity for the team. Last year each of the videos had over a hundred thousand views, and the live shows sell out the Murat every year. It draws a bigger crowd than the traveling Broadway series."

A hundred thousand? A sold out theater?

Some athletes reveled in over exposure. Craved it even. But Deacon Bailey wasn't one of them.

Especially not at this less than pristine moment in his life. A time when he was questioning his own sanity.

"That's still too much. I can't handle that many prying eyes," Deacon replied.

"You have something to hide, Bailey?" Stella's sharp stare slanted in his direction.

Deacon swallowed the tension building in his throat. "No."

"Then what's the problem?"

"I hate being the center of attention," Deacon replied.

"Even if it benefits the local education foundation?" Stella paced closer to the athlete. "They fund the summer lunch program for the inner city schools, run the Fit Kid after school clubs, provide scholarships to students in underserved communities—"

Of course, Stella would play to Deacon's weakness. She had a knack for handling people and pointing them in the direction she most desired.

"I get it," Deacon said, holding up his palm. "You know I'm a sucker for helping others."

But what about aiding his own cause?

Single in the City fans were well known for being over the top. There was no way Deacon could keep fooling around with Reagan while under their scrutinizing lens.

But how the hell was he supposed to stop seeing her? The last few months had proven he didn't have the will power to stay away from her magnetic pull.

In truth, he didn't want to.

Yet, he had to. For Miller's sake.

Perhaps the Single Series was the intervention that would finally do the trick? Goodness knows his own methods hadn't been effective.

Plus, Deacon didn't believe in coincidences. The universe placed this opportunity in his lap for a reason, so he'd be naïve not to pursue her chosen path.

"So you'll do it?" Stella asked, a winning gleam flashing in her amber eyes.

"Yeah." Glancing to Reagan, whose face had paled, Deacon nodded. "I'm in."

The moment the words escaped his lips, Reagan's chair screeched over another round of applause, and her tennis shoes made haste for the bar. Her pursed lips and stony eyes made no secret about her dislike of Deacon's response.

Though Deacon wasn't surprised. Hypersensitive to betrayal, Reagan often overreacted to perceived disloyalty. But deep down, she had to understand his reasoning.

They couldn't be more than friends, and they both knew pursuing anything more would lead to nothing but trouble. Their previous attempts had proven as much.

Moving on was the only option.

Still, her scornful glare cut at his heart.

"What's wrong with her?" Miller leaned toward Kate as he nodded toward his sister who slumped over the bar.

"Hard to say." Kate forced a smile as she squeezed Miller's arm. "I'm sure it's nothing."

Miller's free hand smoothed his tee shirt. "Doesn't seem like nothing."

"Women," Deacon replied with a shrug, pretending he didn't understand what plagued Reagan.

Miller shifted his attention to his friend slapping a hand to his shoulder. "Pretty soon, you're going to have to manage five at once. What do you think about that?"

Deacon took a swig of ale and pushed a tense smile.

Six technically.

But instead of trying to score a shot he could never make, Deacon was going to meet new women and get Reagan Cassidy out of his system.

Chapter Three

"**Y**OU look like you could use one of these." Kate's hand held out a bottle of beer as her jeans lowered to the seat beside Reagan.

An hour after Stella's big announcement, she was still hiding from the crowd of Panthers who were reveling in Deacon's celebration.

"It's been a long year," Reagan sighed, taking the glass container from Kate's grasp and tipping the top to her lips.

"It's only March," Kate noted, her statement soaring over the sounds of the jukebox.

Jaw clenched, Reagan replied, "I know."

Despite the fact that spring was just settling over Indianapolis, Reagan felt as if she'd lived a decade of experiences within the last few months.

Kate's gaze shifted to the herd of towering athletes huddled around Deacon. "I'd ask if your problem is work related, but we both know it's not, so I suppose there's no reason to pretend."

"Just because you know... what you know," Reagan said, scanning the area to see who was within earshot. "That doesn't mean you know everything about my life."

"I know more than most," Kate replied, pulling a few kernels of popcorn from the paper bag sitting in front of Reagan.

"By accident."

A few months prior, knowing Miller was out of town, Reagan caved to the temptation of a late night meeting with Deacon. They'd held strong on their independent pledges to stay apart for near to six months, but something about the falling snow and cooling temperature drove them to desire warmth. Specifically in the form of each other.

Little did Reagan know, her brother had given his new girlfriend a key to his apartment, along with the authority to come and go as she pleased. An ill-timed arrival on Deacon's part let Kate in on their not so little secret.

Not that Reagan was surprised. Her life never zipped down the easy road.

"Accident or not, it's an important piece of information to have." Kate pushed a mahogany lock behind her ear. "It lets me know why you're way over here and not celebrating with everyone else."

"I don't care about Deacon agreeing to do that stupid dating game. The whole concept is ridiculous."

"Then why did you storm away from him the moment he agreed to participate?"

"It was a coincidence," Reagan replied as her finger traced the rim of her glass. "I just happened to need another drink."

"You could have asked the waitress," Kate said.

"The bar is faster," Reagan replied.

Kate's thin lips pursed in silent reflection as her head swayed in disagreement. "Like I said the night I found out, I'm not going to say anything to Miller, so you don't have to put up a front with me."

"I'm not." Reagan tossed her long tresses behind her shoulder and put on her most serious face. She didn't care for the doubt swimming amidst Kate's eyes. "I'm glad for him. We can't become more than a fling, so Deacon may as well take the opportunity to meet someone who can make him happy long term."

"You're assuming you can't be anything more. You haven't actually talked to Miller to know how he feels about it."

Reagan's stare widened. "No, *you* don't know how he feels about it. I've been there, lived that."

Unlike Kate, Reagan had been by Miller's side during his dark days. The rookie years he'd struggled to overcome the corrupt reputation she'd caused.

She'd watched him shoulder the slanderous whispers of strangers. Listened to the people of their suburban hometown berate the athlete who was once their hero. Watched Miller slink into back of the room booths at restaurants to avoid the public's cutting eye.

Reagan's glance moved to her brother who was now laughing with his teammates and enjoying the lighter side of life. His green eyes sparkled with a joy that masked his past woes. But Reagan hadn't forgotten. And despite Miller's newfound happiness, neither had he.

"Trust me when I say he would freak out."

"Maybe you're right. Maybe he wouldn't take it well." Kate conceded with open palms. "But I know what it's like to push a man away for the sake of someone else, and it's not as simple as you're making it seem."

Reagan's lips pursed. "I'm not dense. I know it will be hard to watch him move on, but I can't be selfish again, so I'm choosing to be optimistic. Deacon always says positive energy brings positive energy."

Kate's nose flared. "And your boyfriend dating other women brings the jealousy of your boyfriend dating other women."

"He's *not* my boyfriend." Reagan's body shot up and her jeans shifted against the padded seat as she debated a possible escape from Kate's unrelenting censure. "We've never even been on a real date."

"Maybe not." Kate's fingers combed through her long locks. "But judging by the way you just reacted to the news of the dating show, I think you care enough to raise a few sparks of jealousy when you see Deacon cuddling up to other women. It won't be easy to watch."

Reagan's tennis shoe tapped a beat against the concrete floor. "Men have dealt me worse hands over the years."

Her father's departure when she was a toddler dug a deep scar on her heart, not to mention the turmoil she watched her mother suffer as she tried to raise two young children on her own. All because she'd never realized the fickleness of male feelings.

His roguish version of love left her mother with two jobs and piles of bills, so it was no wonder soft sobs often echoed throughout their small house after the lights had been turned off for the evening.

"Miller has shared a bit about your dad, and I know you two didn't have an easy go of it growing up, but don't sacrifice a good man because you fear he'll hurt you, too. I promise they aren't all the same." Kate squeezed Reagan's arm in a show of support.

"I'm a Cassidy," Reagan scoffed, tugging away from Kate's grasp. "I'm not afraid of anything."

Kate pulled her hand over to her drink. "Based on what I've seen, you're terrified of love. You care for people like a doting nurse, but you always draw the line before things get too intense."

"I'm not afraid of love. I just don't believe in it," Reagan argued, taking a sip from her glass.

"Oh yeah?" Kate's brow rose. "Prove it. Talk to Deacon about the dating show and tell me you feel absolutely nothing when he talks about dating other women."

"Jealousy isn't love," Reagan snipped.

"It still means something," Kate replied. "And you won't be at peace until you know what it implies."

Was Kate right? Was her jealousy blanketing more serious feelings for Deacon?

"I . . . well, umm—"

Kate's torso leaned toward Reagan. "Thought you weren't afraid?"

"I'm not," Reagan snipped once more.

But the armor of assurance she projected only covered her exterior. Inside, Reagan's stomach churned like a blender. Deacon's ability to make her heart flutter stirred her emotions unlike anything she'd ever experienced.

She loved his kindness.

His understanding.

And giving nature.

So much so, Reagan could envision herself falling for him.

Hard.

And that's what made Deacon dangerous.

He had qualities that could blur her memory of him walking away that night at the hotel. And a lowered guard would make her susceptible to the kind of hurt she'd shielded herself from for years.

"It's just talking. What's the worst that could happen?" Kate questioned, taking a sip of her drink.

Reagan's fingers fiddled with her straw.

She could fall for Deacon and ruin everything.

Including her heart.

Chapter Four

METAL vibrated under her fist as Reagan, with the encouragement of a few beverages, pounded on the thick door of Deacon's downtown loft for a third time. Upon Kate's insistence, she'd made her way to Deacon's place to talk, but the flight attendant still wasn't sure what she was going to say.

She was angry.

Annoyed.

Aroused.

Apprehensive.

Anxious.

And that was only the start of the alphabet.

Reagan was twisted between wanting to kiss Deacon and strangle him all at the same time.

He was beautiful, kind, and endearing, but the somber reality was that in accepting a spot as the Single Series bachelor, Deacon had proven that he, like every other man on the planet, could flip flop feelings in a matter of minutes and feel no remorse for doing so.

Not that Reagan was surprised by his actions. Deacon had done the very same thing the night they'd first kissed in Atlanta. He'd embraced her with a fiery passion, and then disappeared faster than a flash of lighting.

"Open up, you hypocrite."

This was why Reagan didn't do romantic relationships any more. Men were unreliable. She'd learned that lesson time and time again.

A creak sounded as the barrier swung open to reveal the athlete clad in black athletic shorts. Fresh from a shower, his bare torso glistened with drops that hadn't yet been touched by a towel.

Well defined muscles rippled down Deacon's front, dipping into a vee at his hips. Taking in the Chinese symbol for wisdom that peeked above his low waistband, Reagan sucked in a sharp breath.

Damn his chiseled chest for attempting to turn her frustration into desire.

"You suck," Reagan hissed.

It wasn't the cutting retort she'd drafted on her way to his apartment, but it shared the same general message of her unhappiness.

"Good to see you, too," Deacon said, running a snowy cloth over his head.

Pushing past his half-naked form, Reagan stormed into Deacon's spacious apartment, her white sneakers soaring across antique wood planks.

Bricks lined the twelve foot wall surrounding the stone fireplace that crackled with low flames. A single can light shining over the kitchen counter highlighted the clean, white walls that lined the rest of the space. The warm air and the gentle glow would have been romantic if she hadn't been so irritated.

"You're really something, you know that?" Reagan said, arms crossing her fitted tee as she paused near the warmth of the hearth.

"Why do I get the sense that you don't mean that as a good thing?" Deacon ran the towel over his upper body once more before tossing it across the back of the leather high back chair.

As always, the athlete's voice was calm and he remained unruffled by her flustered state. Why did he have to be so damn congenial while she was trying to fight?

"Don't play coy. You lied to me," Reagan snipped.

Deacon's brow wrinkled as he took a few strides toward his guest. "How so?"

Reagan huffed, "You've been coming onto me for months and pretending like you wanted to be with me."

"You know damn well I wasn't pretending." Deacon scoffed as his hands pulled her hips flush with his.

The lightweight material of his shorts did little to hide his interest, so he hadn't lied on that count. Deacon's body wanted her. There was no denying that.

But what about his heart? His head? Did they find her desirable as well?

If so, wouldn't he have found a way out of doing the show?

Reagan's scorn-filled eyes met the athlete's gaze. "Then why did you agree to do the dating show?"

Deacon's brow furrowed. "What other choice did I have?"

"You could have said no," Reagan snipped.

"Why?" Deacon's arms opened to the lengthy loft. "We've agreed time and time again that we can't be together because of Miller."

"We can't."

Deacon's eyes widened with frustration. "So what was I supposed to do? Piss off Stella and wait around indefinitely on a chance that our circumstances might change?"

"Yes. No." Reagan heaved a burdened breath as her lashes fluttered shut. "I don't know."

Damn if Deacon wasn't right. She couldn't expect him to move on *and* wait. Or jeopardize his career for a maybe.

But there had to be a better way than this. A reality show was too much. And it was happening too fast.

"You don't like it right now, but deep inside you know becoming the bachelor was the correct choice," Deacon said. "We've brainstormed every scenario and found no positive outcome, so better to rip off the Band-Aid, right?"

"I'm more inclined to soak in a bath to loosen the adhesive," she replied.

"You know what I mean."

Reagan's lashes lowered. "I didn't expect you to wait forever, but I thought you might give it a little longer to see if we could figure something out."

"If there were an obvious answer, we would have found it by now." Moving away from Reagan, the athlete sank to the couch in defeat. "Besides, you know as well as I do that Stella doesn't take no for an answer. Once she gets an idea in her head, there's no changing her mind."

"There's a first time for everything," Reagan replied, her finger trailed the concrete mantle as she strolled the length of the hearth.

Deacon's head tilted as an unusual pessimism radiated from his eyes. "Not with Stella."

Reagan paused as her gaze pierced the athlete. "So this is it? You're doing the dating show and we're moving on? For real this time?"

"It appears the universe has spoken," Deacon said, looping an arm over a pillow. "With the same message as usual."

"Stay apart." Reagan's tone softened as she settled next to Deacon, her hands wedging between her legs.

Deacon's palm covered her thigh. "Unfortunately."

Sadness settled on his face, while a similar dreariness tugged at Reagan's chest.

They'd attempted to find a loophole in the hard truth, but such a thing didn't exist. Life wasn't a game where everyone could win. Someone had to reign victorious, and in this instance, that person had to be Miller.

Though, it wasn't as if she and Deacon had to say goodbye forever. Once they overcame their infatuation, the two could settle back into their former routine.

They'd formed an unlikely closeness four years prior when Miller joined the Panther's roster, bonding first over a love of books and travel. Their attachment growing over movie nights and her nursing Deacon back to health after surgery. Surely, they could find that again?

Camaraderie was a silver lining in need of polish, but it was better than nothing.

"After things cool off, we can go back to being friends," Reagan said, reassuring herself as much as him.

Deacon's dismal gaze shifted her direction. "Most people would say they'd rather be a friend than be nothing at all, but I'm not sure I can do that. Not with you."

Reagan's thick lashes fluttered with confusion. "You don't want to see me anymore?"

"I want to be near you all the time. That's the problem," Deacon said, looping a fallen strand of hair behind her ear before tipping her chin up. "I don't know how to be with you and not be *with* you."

"It will take some adjusting," Reagan said, her pulse picking up at the graze of his fingers. "But I guess we'll figure it out. Thanks to Stella, we don't really have a choice now, do we?"

"Unless you're willing to confess all to Miller, and let the cards fall where they may, we can only muddle through until we get to the other side," Deacon said, brushing his hand over her back.

"Until one of us meets someone else who makes us forget," Reagan said, turning to the athlete.

"I suppose," Deacon replied, not meeting her gaze.

A knowing silence settled between them.

He would move on first, and they both recognized that fact. The dating show would provide Deacon with beautiful women who were screened with his taste in mind. Beauty, charm, intelligence, the contestants would have it all. With no brother to stand in the way.

"Do you think you'll fall for one of the women on the show?"

"I don't know," Deacon shrugged, pulling Reagan to his chest. "The contestants won't be you, so that's a strike against them."

Reagan's palm cupped his tawny cheek with gentle reverence. "They'll probably be better."

"Not likely," Deacon replied, pulling her soft hand to his lips.

His smooth kiss caressed up her bare arm, only pausing when blocked by her cap sleeve. Skipping over the cloth, Deacon nipped at the curve of her neck.

Reagan clipped Deacon's advance with the slight tilt of her head, but undeterred, he continued his pursuit to her jaw.

"Maybe one of them will like those terrible westerns you love to watch." Fighting the melting sensation coursing through her veins, Reagan attempted to hold strong against the athlete's tantalizing touch. "And I'm sure one will know how to cook something other than frozen pizza. Which is more than I can say."

"I don't want to think about any of that right now," Deacon said, his lips taking a slow drag off of hers like she was a fine cigar he wanted to relish. "I'd rather just enjoy a few quiet hours with you while we can. What do you think?"

A gulp wound down Reagan's throat.

No. She should say no.

Their first full night together couldn't be their last.

It would be too hard.

And something always went wrong.

But Reagan's usual fear of being discovered lessened in the safe haven of Deacon's apartment. After all, what could possibly go wrong in the private confines of his home?

Surely, nothing of significance.

Perhaps tonight was the closure she and Deacon required in order to advance to their new chapters?

Once they had each other, the thrill of the chase would subside, and they would be able to move on.

Wouldn't they?

Drawn like a magnet to metal, Reagan's mouth pressed a kiss to the athlete's bare shoulder.

With Deacon's intoxicating kiss clouding her mind, she couldn't muster enough fight to leave anyways. Not when they didn't have much time left together.

Running her hands across his chest, Reagan explored his taut, brown skin. Influenced by her touch, his breath became labored, while the lids of his eyes grew heavy with want. A need she understood as desire vibrated through every cell in her body.

A wicked grin lit Reagan's face as she settled on her decision to stay. "I hope it doesn't have to be *too* quiet this evening."

Transforming his somber stare, a wolfish gleam sparked from Deacon's eyes. "I could probably get over a little clamoring."

Reagan lifted from her seated position and began to back toward the hallway where the bedrooms were located. As she stepped, her fingers popped the silver button atop her jeans. Zipper lowered, her thumbs pushed at her waistband. First, with a teasing dip. Then, she sent the denim spilling to the wood floor. Turning back toward Deacon, her right brow rose in a dare.

"Only a little?"

♥

DEACON'S PALM CLUTCHED his chest as Reagan revealed painted on black boy shorts. Contrasting from the white tee that drooped at her waist, lacy edges framed her creamy curves. Hips wavering as if music was playing, Reagan urged Deacon to follow her path. As if he needed more encouragement. She was the drug the athlete couldn't quit.

No doubt, like most illegal substances, Reagan was going to be the death of him, or perhaps the death of his friendship with Miller. But in the moment, Deacon didn't care. Drowning in the sweet scent of his vixen would be worth whatever punishment followed.

Leaping from the couch, Deacon pinned Reagan's back to the wall in five seconds flat. His fingers wound through the soft waves cascading to her shoulders as his mouth covered hers.

"Is your main goal in life to drive me crazy?" he rumbled.

Embracing the captive state, Reagan's pelvis ground against the thigh he was using to hold her in place. "I can leave if I'm bothering you."

Deacon's hands cupped her round butt, pulling his lover closer. His eyes roamed the curve of her chest. "Oh, I am definitely bothered."

Lips caressing the soft skin of her neck, bliss coursed through his veins, but the athlete maintained his restraint against taking her that very second. As much as Deacon wanted more than a fling with Reagan, such a future wasn't possible, so he had to revel in what time they had. And he sure as hell wasn't going to leave her with any memory other than the most sensual, pleasure filled night of her life.

"My apologies. I'm kind of known for being a mess," Reagan said, her hand winding to Deacon's waistband.

"You're a *hot* mess," Deacon grinned, nipping at her lips once more.

"But you don't mind the heat, do you?" Reagan said, her touch dipping below the elastic.

Deacon's forehead pressed to hers. "I love it."

He was a moth drawn to her radiant flame. It burned over the melting wax of a candle that would soon fizzle out. But Deacon couldn't allow himself to focus on anything but the positive, so he opted to revel in the need radiating from her touch. The fingers he'd been wrapped around longer than he cared to admit.

Without even trying to, Reagan had penetrated his soft natured soul years ago.

From the moment they met at Miller's apartment, she'd welcomed him into the folds of their little clan as a second brother. Knowing his family was too far out of reach for their limited time off, she always made sure to include Deacon in the Cassidy holiday plans. And even though he'd first been disgusted by the idea of carrots and pineapple floating together in the Jello salad her grandmother adored, he'd come to appreciate Reagan's willingness to please those she loved. Even if it meant choking back a few bites of the strange orange gelatin she mixed for every gathering.

More than that, Reagan wanted to know him as a person and not as an athlete. In fact, she rarely spoke of the sport.

Instead, he and Reagan shared stories about what they hoped for in their futures. Him, a family and a purposeful career after he hung up his high tops, and for her, adventure. They talked about art and books and things his teammates didn't care about. Her meaningful words filled a void missing in his hum drum day to day as a professional athlete. Most people assumed Deacon wanted to talk basketball, but stats, plays, and drills were Deacon's job. They didn't define him as a person. And Reagan saw that.

Saw him. Deacon Bailey. The man beneath the jersey.

As if she sensed his mind slipping from the moment, Reagan's teeth nipped at his lips as her searing fingers trailed to his throbbing groin. Her touch was soft, yet demanding as she caressed him toward the brink of a full on psychosis where his worries melted away.

Deacon's hands cupped the round curve of Reagan's chest,

admiring how the perfect measure of her fullness fit his palms just so. But when he pressed a kiss to her neck, Reagan's warm stroke paused, pulling the athlete from his trance. He ached for her continued massage, but Reagan's upper body stiffened.

"Babe? Is something wrong?" Deacon growled. "Did I hurt you?"

If she said yes, he was going to harm himself for creating even a moment of pain for her. And if it was the universe interrupting once more, he was going to wound whoever she sent to do her bidding.

Reagan nodded to the door as she whispered, "This is the third time they've rang."

They? Who was they?

"What are you talking about?"

Reagan slipped her hand from his waistband and used her palms to cup his face. "The doorbell, Deacon. Someone's here."

Deacon's lids hit a hard double as he tried to refocus his attention. "Who?"

"I don't know. I can't see through metal." Wrinkles creased on Reagan's brow. "It's kind of late for a normal visitor, though. Are you expecting someone?"

"No."

Ignoring the fourth set of bells as he had the others, Deacon's lips refocused their attention on Reagan's neck. He also made a mental note to disable the stupid doorbell the following day.

"Just ignore it. Probably a pizza delivery guy with the wrong address."

Thunder sounded from the door as a heavy hand gave up on the bell and rapped against the metal plank.

"Deacon. I know you're home. I can see the damn lights filtering under the door, and I know you're not the type to leave them on while you're out."

Deacon's heated flesh turned ice cold at the sound of Miller's booming voice.

"What the hell is he doing here?" Reagan's eyes bugged. Her tone matching that of a mother secretly scolding her child in a store. "Did you know he was coming?"

Was she serious?

"Oh, yeah. I thought I'd invite him over so he could witness me seduce his sister," Deacon growled as he pushed away from the wall. "I figured that would be a great bonding experience for us."

Reagan shoulders lifted as she whispered, "You could have made plans you forgot about. It's not like you knew I was coming."

"I know I'm more mature than a lot of the people you've dated, but I'm not actually old. I still have my mind," Deacon replied, tapping his knuckles to his head. "Some of it anyways."

The athlete couldn't deny that he'd obviously lost some of his smarts to land in this precarious position. Hooking up with his best friend's little sister was asking for trouble. But how was he supposed to maintain coherency when Reagan clouded most of his rational thoughts?

Still, he hadn't lost all brain activity. Deacon was aware Miller's presence at his apartment threatened everything they'd worked so hard to keep quiet.

Reagan leaned into Deacon's chest once more as her fingers grazed his chest. "If you didn't invite him, maybe he'll go away."

"Have you met your brother?" Deacon scoffed. "When does he ever back down from a challenge?"

"Deacon. I can hear you mumbling in there. I'm using my emergency key in ten seconds, so you may as well just let me in."

"Told you." Deacon's head tilted as Miller began his slow countdown.

"He has a key?" Reagan mouthed as her fingernails dug into Deacon's arms.

Deacon groaned, "For emergencies."

"This is going to be an emergency if he finds me here," Reagan seethed.

"Go hide in my bedroom," Deacon ordered, spinning Reagan around and nudging her down the long hall. "It's not like he knows to look for you."

"Oh no," Reagan's heels dug into the wood as she turned back to Deacon. Her fingertips wrapped his tee. "What if he does? What if Kate cracked and told him because of the dating show?"

Deacon's heart skipped a beat.

"Then, I'm glad you're here to call an ambulance when he's through with me." Deacon urged Reagan into the master bedroom.

Reagan's right hand caught the door frame. Like bright stars in the night sky, her worried, blue eyes peeked out. "I'm not worth physical injury, Deacon."

"On the contrary." Deacon popped a reverent kiss to her forehead. "You're worth every ounce of pain."

With a crack, the front door flung open, bringing a burst of fluorescent light to the dimly lit apartment. Miller's footsteps creaked over the wood floor as his voice echoed up to the apartments tall ceilings. "What the hell is going on?"

Chapter Five

DEACON flew from the end of the hallway to the main living area, never more grateful for his speed. However, not wanting to further alert Miller that something was amiss, he slowed his pace as he neared the main space.

Calming his heavy breath, the athlete stalked out of the dim corridor just in time to see Miller break the living room's threshold. Dressed down in gray athletic pants and a hunter green tee, his apparel was casual, however the rigid look on his friend's face was anything but mellow. Deacon registered the meaning without difficulty, seeing as Reagan shared the same frustrated tension when she was upset.

Folding his arms, Deacon clipped, "What the hell are you doing here?"

"You seemed on edge when we left Lockerbie's," Miller replied.

"So?" Deacon's question cut the thick air hovering between them.

Miller's fingers shoved a dangling pair of silver keys back into his pocket. "So, I tried to text you to see if you were okay with this whole dating show situation."

"I told you I was fine."

"But you never responded to my text, so I thought I'd stop by after I dropped Kate off and make sure nothing was wrong. I'm not going to have my best friend be the athlete of the week found dead in his apartment because no one bothered to check in on him when he was down."

"I'm fine," Deacon repeated.

"I can see that now," Miller replied, flopping into the lush, red pillows lining the couch. "But for all I knew you were passed out drunk in a gutter."

"It's nearly midnight," Deacon argued, turning back for the main living space, knocking Miller's feet to the ground as he passed to the adjacent recliner. "I could've been asleep."

"But you weren't," Miller replied, wrapping his long arms around the back of the couch. "So why didn't you respond to my text or answer the door? I rang your bell five times."

"Uhh . . ." Deacon should have anticipated that question. Should have thought up a plausible answer ahead of time. "I was . . . uhh . . ." Glancing to the towel draped over his high back chair, Deacon mumbled, ". . . in the shower."

Miller's head slanted as he assessed Deacon's physical state. "You're not wet. At all."

"I dried off."

"In thirty seconds?"

"I don't have floppy, surfer hair like you," Deacon argued, waving to Miller's fluffed pompadour. "And I'm faster in general."

"Lies." Miller said, his eyes scanning the room as if he were an investigator searching for a clue that lead to the truth. "But why?"

He wouldn't find anything, though. Deacon was meticulously clean and organized. Nothing was ever out of place. No clutter. No—

Shit.

Deacon's eyes found what Miller was searching for a single second sooner.

Reagan's pants.

They were puddled on the floor where she'd seductively removed them. In his haste to hide her, Deacon had forgotten to remove the evidence. In his spic and span home, there was no way Miller wouldn't notice them.

The athlete thought living in accordance to Feng Shui would bring peace to his life, but that was turning out to be a disillusion. His home's cleanly state was about to bring a layer of chaos like he'd never known.

When his eyes landed on Reagan's lost apparel, Miller leaned forward, and his green eyes widened with excitement as his blonde brow lifted. "Whose jeans?"

"They're mine," Deacon said, shifting toward the evidence. Perhaps he could toss them aside before Miller noticed they were entirely too small for his thick thighs? "I must have dropped them when I was doing laundry."

"I thought your housekeeper did your laundry?" Miller's head cocked as his eyes slanted.

The teammates held a momentary stare down until Miller made his move. Hopping across the coffee table, the athlete scrambled to scoop up the evidence before Deacon could snatch it away.

Darting as quick as his socked feet would allow, Deacon attempted to thwart Miller's attempt. With a shorter stature, and a few less pounds to carry, Deacon always bested Miller in sprints at practice. Surely, he could do it now. When it mattered most of all.

But this time, Deacon's speed was no match Miller's height. His friend's long arms reached for the clothing, whisking it from Deacon's grasp. A victorious gleam lit Miller's face as he balled the clothing and pivoted away from his friend's swatting palm.

"Top notch rebounding at its finest," Miller smirked. His left arm poised in a defensive stance as his right arm angled up and away from his opposition.

"You're a jerk," Deacon snuffed, wiping a sweat bead from his brow in a fake out before leaping for the pants.

"And you're not?" Miller replied, blocking Deacon's advance. "When the hell were you going to tell me you've got some side chick?"

"It's not like that," Deacon said, palms running over his buzzed scalp as he accepted defeat.

"The hell it's not. They smell like perfume from a foot away," Miller grinned, chucking the denim to Deacon's chest. "Plus, I know they belong to a woman because Reagan has a pair exactly like that. Red stitches on the pockets and all."

Deacon's face dropped at the mention of her name. In response, Miller's gleam dampened and his eyes narrowed.

"In fact, she's had them for a long time. A pair exactly like that. Only hers—"

With swift fury, Miller's hands tugged the pants from Deacon's grasp. His fingers found the small tag sewn in the back of the waistband. The athlete's jaw grew rigid as he maneuvered the small flap to find Reagan's initials scrawled with a Sharpie. Deacon had suggested she do so after she voiced concerns about her clothes getting mixed up with her sorority sisters' apparel. Now, watching the fire build in Miller's eyes, Deacon realized it was the worst idea he'd ever had.

"You have about five seconds to explain why the hell my sister's jeans are on your floor."

Chapter Six

INTERNALLY screaming at her neglect, Reagan's palm slapped her forehead.

How could she have forgotten to pick up the stupid pants?

Why had she even come to Deacon's apartment in the first place?

Months of caution and sacrifice were about to be thrown out the window all because of a simple mistake.

At the very end of it all, no less.

A bead of sweat formed on Reagan's brow as she heard Miller's voice bellow with anger. So much for her brother not piecing together the puzzle. With all the clues they'd thrown him, why wouldn't he suspect foul play?

Unless . . . Reagan sucked in a hopeful breath. Unless, she gave her brother more pieces to play with. Pieces that didn't fit the narrative he expected to hear. Pieces that changed what the final picture looked like.

Head poking out from the door frame, she tugged on a pair of Deacon's compression shorts. Reagan peered down the hall to where Deacon was frozen in place. Miller's fist gripped the neck of his t-shirt like a vice as his towering body arched over his prey. Shadows sculpted Deacon's panicked expression, emphasizing he had no game plan.

Left to his own devices, Deacon would tell the truth.

Then, Miller would throw the pending blow he'd cocked ten seconds prior.

And that would be the beginning of the end for all of their relationships.

Reagan had to intervene. Had to show herself. It was the only way to keep their secret and prevent another of her brother's relationships from suffering from her whims.

It was a huge risk, but Miller had already come to the worst conclusion. So could she really make things worse?

"Calm down," Reagan snipped with false bravado, exiting from her hiding place.

Black Lycra hugged her previously bare legs as she shoved Miller away from Deacon.

"It's not what you think."

At least, she hoped she could convince Miller the scenario was far different from what it seemed. As a flight attendant, Reagan put on a show for passengers every day while wrangling them from agitated states. Surely, she could work her charms on her brother.

Despite Deacon's scrunched face doubting her mission, Reagan had to believe she could slow their rambling train before it sped off course.

Un-balling the denim material, Miller stretched the pants to reveal the incriminating initials on the tag.

"So I didn't just find my sister's pants discarded on my best friend's floor after he was unreachable for an hour? When I know she's been sneaking around with someone?"

Reagan waved off her brother's concern as she paused by Deacon's side. "Why am I not surprised that you're jumping to irrational conclusions? You're always such a hot head, overreacting before you know the whole story."

"Given the circumstances I think I'm completely justified in suspecting that you two are... are..." Miller's fingers met his reddened forehead as his anguished face tilted to the ceiling. "I can't even say it. But you know what you're doing."

"Oh no, you figured it out." Reagan's voice oozed with sarcasm as she pulled her left hand to her heart. Batting her lashes with excessive force, she wrapped her free palm around Deacon's bicep and posed, staring at her partner as if they were on the cover of a romance novel. "Our secret has been revealed, my love."

Deacon's dark eyes widened with fear and excitement. Breathless, Deacon muttered, "What are you doing?"

Lifting her voice again, the young woman continued with her mockery, pulling her chest flush with the athlete's. "Miller, it's time you know. Deacon and I are in love, and we've decided we're getting married."

"Married?" Miller bellowed. "You can't be serious."

"Our connection was written in the stars years ago, so don't try to separate us, dear brother. For we couldn't bear to be apart." Reagan accented her final statement by flinging the back of her hand to her head and crumbling in an over exaggerated faint.

Deacon's muscled arms caught her fall, and she was thankful for his quick reflexes.

"You're being ridiculous," Miller grimaced, his fingers combing his sandy pompadour. "You two being together . . . it wouldn't make any sense. I know you have this weird friendship, but you're polar opposites."

Reagan scoffed internally as Deacon righted her stance. Miller was so caught up in seeing her as the little girl she once was, that he'd missed the part where she grew up and gained new interests. She wasn't the irresponsible, thoughtless creature she'd once been.

Pushing away from Deacon's side, Reagan strolled to her brother. Glaring up at Miller, she snatched her jeans from his grip. "So what are you flipping out about?"

Miller's long arms opened to the living room. "You have to admit that this situation looks more than a little suspicious."

"The pants are a joke," Reagan said, her hand flipping to the expanse of Deacon's loft. "This place is a museum, so after changing I threw the pants on the floor to feel a little more at home. You know I thrive in chaos. Plus, it's kind of fun to get under his skin." Reagan's palm pushed a playful shove at Deacon's bicep.

"Always the rebel," Deacon muttered.

Miller's face stayed flat as his arms folded across his chest. Assessing eyes darted from Reagan to Deacon and then back to his sister again. "That still doesn't explain why you're here in the first place."

Reagan sighed, her back falling to the plush couch. She and Deacon had been lying for so long that the fibs rolled off her tongue without effort.

"The guy I'm seeing got called in to work last minute, so I asked Deacon if I could hang out here for a little while. My pants were tight and uncomfortable, so I borrowed some of his shorts. Thankfully, Spandex makes for universal sizing."

Matching her move, Miller lowered to the recliner. His face was still hardened with disbelief. "Why wouldn't you come to my apartment? Remember, that place where you have your own room with an attached bath."

"It's a Jack and Jill that I share with Kai," Reagan chaffed.

A hint of guilt tugged at Reagan's conscience. She loved Miller's spunky mentee, and since they had double sinks, sharing wasn't really a chore. But afraid her brother might see the truth, Reagan had to point a finger at someone else before he stared too long in her direction.

"So?"

"There are rainbow colored fish on the shower curtain," she

continued, grappling for something to complain about.

"We both know you let him pick out the decorations." Miller's elbows met his thighs. "So what's really going on? Why are you here?"

"Deac and I are friends, you know that."

"Yeah, but I can tell there's more to your story," Miller argued.

"Stop meddling. Just let me live my life." Pulling a cushion from behind her back, Reagan launched the padded square at Miller's head, but he captured the projectile before it made contact with anything of consequence.

Damn his quick hands.

"As your older brother, it's my job to protect you," Miller said, flipping the pillow to his side.

"Then protect, don't snoop."

"I'm not. Kate's the one who is overly nosy. Not me." A knowing realization settled on her brother's face. "This wouldn't have something to do with her . . . would it?"

Winging her plan at the last minute, Reagan hadn't considered playing that angle, but blaming Kate was the perfect excuse. Although, she hated to blame the person who had willingly risked the trust built in her relationship with Miller to keep their secret.

"I think she's nice, and I'm glad you're happy," Reagan said. "But it's awkward as hell when we're both at your apartment."

Miller chucked the pillow back at his sister, hitting her square in the chest. "She's my girlfriend. What do you want me to do? Tell her she can't come over?"

"Of course not," Reagan replied, arms wrapping the pillow instead of sending it soaring back. "But when she's there, I can't help but feel like I'm intruding on your personal time. Not to mention, she's bossy, so we're tug of warring over who gets to be queen of the hive and decide if the coffee pods should be left on the counter or in the cabinet."

"A little organization never hurt anyone."

"It's way more convenient when the pods are already out in a spinning rack. No one has the energy to sort through those little boxes early in the morning." Reagan kicked her bare feet up on the coffee table. "Everyone who actually drinks coffee knows that."

"Kate is just trying to help," Miller defended. "She wants you to like her."

"And I want the same," Reagan said. "Which is why we need to spend less nights cohabitating."

"I suppose you have a point, but you could've just told me." Miller leaned back in the chair as he pointed to Deacon. "You, too."

"I didn't want you to worry about it," Reagan said. "You have enough on your plate, and I can take care of myself."

Miller had sacrificed too many of his teenage years trying to be the father figure she needed. Reagan didn't want him to give up his twenties, too. She wanted her brother to see that she was capable of finding her way through the world on her own. An independent woman, Reagan didn't *need* a hovering man to make her feel secure any longer.

Wanting though, that was becoming a different issue altogether. Reagan's body wanted Deacon like she'd never wanted anything before.

She craved his touch.

His kiss.

Him.

But her sensible brain knew desire was temporary. Like all good things, it was bound to fade with time. A want wasn't stable.

Minds changed. People changed. And rarely for the better in romantic relationships.

Reagan figured out long ago that the smartest thing a woman could ever do was not *need* a man, and she wasn't about to relearn that lesson.

Chapter Seven

CLOSING the door behind Miller, Deacon's shoulders slumped with relief as he turned back for the living room. "Do you think he believed your little tale?"

Reagan's heart still pulsed with anxiety over the near catch, but she nodded her affirmation. Their secret was safe for now.

"Miller wouldn't have let me stay if he didn't," she confirmed.

Always playing the role of protective big brother, Miller would have drug her out kicking and screaming if he felt it was in her best interest.

"Good point," Deacon said, falling to the couch beside Reagan, whose feet were now propped on the coffee table. "Though I'm not sure I care for how quickly he jumped to the conclusion that we don't make sense together."

"He doesn't understand how we have a friendship without a lot of shared interest," Reagan said.

From Miller's view, she was flighty where Deacon was reliable.

Her temper was quick to boil, while Deacon was calm and collected in all circumstances.

He came from a happy family, and she came from divorced parents.

"How can he say we have nothing in common when he knows we

both like pineapple on pizza?" Deacon's jaw dropped in false offense as he rolled to his side.

"I can't believe he forgot such a big one," Reagan chuckled.

Coming from a home where there wasn't a lot of laughter, she appreciated Deacon's lightheartedness in the midst of stress. It was nice, that even moments of strain, he could put a smile on his face and reassure her that it would all be okay. He was one of a kind in that way. And so many others.

"Don't roll your eyes. We both know there's other stuff, too," Deacon said, his hand wrapping her stomach as his thumb brushed against her cotton shirt. "We both enjoy travel. Appreciate a good book. And there's this . . ."

Deacon lowered his lips to hers with gentle reverence. As if either of them could forget they had that connection.

"Chemistry," Reagan sighed.

"Bubbling like a cylinder in science class," Deacon said.

If only that were enough to sustain a future.

"A lot of those experiments erupt and make a huge mess."

Deacon's teeth tugged at her lower lip as he rolled atop Reagan's body and pinned her to the couch. His thighs hugged her hips with transcendent tension. Meeting his demand her pelvis arched with want.

"Erupt, really?" the athlete groaned. "You cannot use such a word unless you intend to do something about it."

Peering into Deacon's glittering gaze, Reagan wanted to throw inhibition to the wind. Wanted to do what felt right instead of what was right.

But she couldn't.

She had to think of Miller. Had to do right by him this time.

Though five years had passed, she'd never forgiven herself for ruining Miller's oldest friendship and his reputation.

He'd bonded with Brandon at Kindergarten orientation, and

they were inseparable from that moment on, spending an inordinate amount of time at each other's houses and playing basketball on the same team from elementary to high school. In a sense, Brandon had been Reagan's second older brother—until the day he wasn't.

A drunken college party, and lowered inhibitions, shifted comfort and familiarity to lust and longing. And once the switch flipped, there was no going back.

At the beginning of Reagan's relationship with Brandon, her brother had been reluctant to accept them as a couple. In all fairness, she'd never been a big believer in long term commitment, so his concern was warranted. But over the course of a few months, the trio settled in to their new normal with their new roles. Miller even seemed pleased that they were happy together.

But a few months later, when Brandon cheated on Reagan at a frat party, a feisty, young Miller had been quick to confront the wrongdoing. Unfortunately, his retribution took place on the court when their teams played the following week. Brandon suffered a broken nose while Miller received four stitches on his chin.

After that, the two never spoke again.

Not when Brandon's mom died. Not when Miller was drafted to the pros.

Never.

Worst of all, Miller's epic throw down with Brandon was the moment he gained his notorious status for fighting.

All because Reagan had given in to lust.

Because she'd trusted love.

Reagan's lids lowered. "Deacon, you know I can't."

"But earlier—"

Pushing Deacon's muscled body to the side, Reagan sat up before she lost her conviction. Another second under his herculean form and she was likely to give way to her desire.

"We were about to make a huge mistake, so the universe interrupted."

"Miller coming here was a coincidence." Deacon reached for Reagan's bicep and attempted to pull her close once more.

Pulling away from the athlete's grasp, Reagan lifted to her feet and made her way to the fireplace. Her arms crossed as she paced. "You don't believe in coincidences. And it's only a fluke if it happens once. But every time we try to get together, something goes wrong or someone interferes. That has to mean something."

Deacon swept behind Reagan, wrapping his arms around her thin frame. "Maybe it means that we should stop keeping secrets and come out with the truth."

Reagan sighed.

As if telling the truth would improve their circumstances. For a man so wise, Deacon was green when it came to understanding the inner workings of relationships. Especially when it came to Miller.

Reagan's head shook in disagreement. "Miller would be paranoid the entire time we were dating. He'd go crazy and drive us mad in the process."

"Unless he knew it was serious." Deacon unwrapped Reagan and spun her to face him.

Reagan held up her left hand and wiggled her fingers. "Nothing short of marriage would convince Miller of that."

"And you don't believe in marriage," Deacon replied, merging his palm to hers.

Reagan's lashes lifted as she met the athlete's fierce gaze. He was a great person, but no man was worth the risk of marriage.

"Not in the slightest," she said.

"So we've circled around to right where we are." Deacon's eyes rose to the ceiling. "Stuck in hiding."

"We're not stuck," Reagan said, resting her hands on the athlete's taut chest. "You're going to be the Single in the City bachelor, and we're both going to move on."

The flight attendant had plans to rise with the pink streaks of sunrise and set off on a mid-day departure to Paris. Going to the city of love wasn't her ideal destination, but it was the furthest she'd been able to get with such short notice. Fill-in spots to Europe were never on the market long, so she'd jumped on the opportunity before someone else snatched it up. Reagan needed space to process all that had transpired over the last few days.

She'd always known she and Deacon couldn't be together, but accepting the reality that he was going to date other women was proving more difficult than expected.

Sure, she was always disappointed when her relationships ended, but not a believer in marriage or love, Reagan knew a breakup was the inevitable outcome. There was no other choice.

But this time, with Deacon, it was more than a melancholy moment. Leaving him behind felt like an actual loss.

He made Reagan wished she did believe in happily ever after. That she were less jaded. Especially when she saw the sincerity that streamed from his warm eyes.

She wondered what her life might have been if she hadn't come from a broken home. If, like Deacon, she had two loving parents in a happy marriage. If her brother's happiness and career weren't at stake.

Reagan laid her flushed cheek to Deacon's chest.

Pondering such ideas was a waste of time. Doing so wouldn't change her circumstances.

Miller would never accept them.

And Reagan would never be fool enough to fall in love.

Chapter Eight

A SOFT glow of city street lights filtered through the bamboo blinds covering Deacon's guest room windows. Unable to sleep, he stood in the doorway and studied the shadows that framed Reagan's peaceful face. Sleeping starfish style, she took up more than her fair share of a king size bed. If they ever found their way together, he'd be relegated to a slender foot on the edge of the mattress.

But a lack of personal space wasn't what troubled the athlete.

No. The issues lurking bedside were bigger than a bad night's sleep.

He'd suggested facing their problem head on by telling Miller the truth about their feelings, and Reagan had blown off his idea. Deacon was aware of her inherent distrust of men, and her overall disbelief in love, but it appeared the hurt her father left behind ran deeper than he previously thought.

On top of that, his best friend had been quick to disregard Reagan's confession of love as a hoax. Granted, she'd engaged her inner smart-alek during the dramatic declaration, but was the idea of them together that unbelievable?

Deacon could admit that their personalities were different, but opposites were known to attract. And they had plenty in common.

Like basketball.

The firm belief that eggs should always have a runny yellow in which to dip toast.

The athlete's brain was too rattled from the evening's events to make a definitive list, but there was more than enough to keep them happy for many years.

He hadn't been certain it was possible before. Had thought it was best to go their separate ways for Miller's sake.

But once Deacon found himself in the position where he believed his friend had found out the truth, he realized the gain outweighed the consequence.

Unfortunately, Reagan didn't view the situation with the same lens. She was too afraid. Unable to see beyond her own experiences to realize that relationships could bring more than damage to a person's life.

As if Reagan that wasn't enough for Deacon to worry about, she'd barely protested his participating in the dating show.

Sure, the idea had her heated for a few hours, but she'd calmed down relatively quick once they'd talked. He'd convinced her to see reason.

Any other woman would have been jealous as hell at the simple mention of the idea. So why wasn't Reagan?

She'd never said she loved him, nor had he shared such a phrase with her, but Deacon had felt the radiance of affection flow from her lips. At least, he thought he had.

Perhaps he'd been deceived?

Reagan *had* put on an impressive show for Miller. Even knowing the truth, Deacon almost believed her tale. Which led him to wonder, had she performed a similar act for him?

Had she lied to him about her feelings?

Was he just a form of entertainment for her?

Given Reagan's insistence on hiding their feelings from Miller, and her current interest in parting ways, it wasn't an implausible idea.

Because when someone met their soulmate, didn't they want to shout it from the rooftops? Even if it meant going against a brother and a good friend's wishes, didn't they want the world to know?

And what did it mean if they didn't?

Chapter Nine

THE following Friday, post-game interviews complete, Deacon carried his tired muscles to the Panther's locker room where hunter green cubbies lined the wall. His aches called for an ice bath, but his head, and the rest of his body, desired warmth. Specifically in the form of a fetching female.

Not that those desires would be met. Reagan had shipped out on a last minute, weeklong European stint the day after Stella's announcement. No doubt, she was trying to avoid him. Avoid them and the trouble that seemed to follow.

Deacon tugged his damp, white jersey over his head and tossed it to the bottom of his locker.

"You okay, man?" Miller's cotton towel snapped at Deacon's carved abs. "You look like shit, and you were playing worse."

"Just sore." Deacon's fingers massaged up and down his arm to help solidify his claim. "I'm not as young as I used to be."

"That's not what I mean," Miller said, tossing the towel over his shoulder. "Ever since Stella announced you were in the damn dating show, something's been off."

"We won, so what does it matter?"

For the sake of speed, and avoiding conversation with Miller, the athlete decided to forgo a shower until he got home. Instead of undressing like many of his teammates, Deacon slipped a Panthers t-shirt over his chiseled chest.

"It matters because we won't make it very far in the playoffs with you in a funk," Miller plopped in his chair and propped his sneakers on Deacon's seat with a thud. "So why don't you tell me what's really going on?"

"It's nothing. Just feeling my age." With a fake groan, Deacon knelt to unlace his game shoes. Even though he wanted to escape the locker room, his fingers worked the ties at a turtle pace.

Over the last nine months of skirting around whatever it was he and Reagan were doing, Deacon had learned the importance of solidifying a story with believable details, so he had to play up his imaginary discomfort.

Not that he enjoyed lying.

In fact, Deacon hated every minute of it.

The athlete wanted to break down the wall of deception built between he and Miller and tell his best friend everything. And not only because the fibs were gnawing at his conscience, but because Deacon needed advice.

Was desperate for it at the moment.

After all, who knew crazed women better than Miller Cassidy?

Years of flings gone wrong had filled him with a lifetime of knowledge on how to handle tricky situations with female counterparts.

"Nothing always means it's a woman." Miller's rigid chin lifted as his green eyes narrowed. "But I thought you weren't dating?"

Deacon's fingers massaged his temples. "Technically, I'm not."

It was a half-truth, but at least it wasn't a whole lie. As far as the world was concerned, he was a single man.

Miller's arms propped behind his head as if he were reclined on a couch. "But you want to be?"

Deacon sighed. This was his chance to lay it all out on the table. An opportunity to tell the truth. But Reagan would be furious if he admitted their crime without her permission, and that worked against Deacon's new goal of convincing her that they could be together without inciting drama in her family life.

Yet, the athlete couldn't fib again. Couldn't look his best friend in the eye and tell and bold faced lie. He had to lift the weight crushing his chest before it caused permanent damage to his spirit.

But was it possible to tell Miller the truth without him growing overly suspicious? Deacon's eyes darted toward Miller, but they found his titled stare curious, not calculating.

Perhaps if he left out some of the details . . .

"Maybe." The athlete's caution caused the vowels to drag.

"So you do have someone on the side." Miller gleamed as he snapped his towel at Deacon once more. "I can't believe you didn't tell me."

"I'm telling you now," Deacon said, swatting at the cracking cloth. "I didn't before because she wants to keep it low key. Or no key. I don't even know."

"She who?" Miller's smile drooped as his back straightened. "Because that sentiment sounds extremely familiar . . . and the other night —"

Deacon cut off Miller's concern with the wave of his hand. "She's someone I used to be friends with. I've known her for a long time."

His forehead scrunching, Miller ground through a tight jaw. "How long?"

"Long enough," Deacon replied, holding up a palm to signal Miller to stop.

"You have to admit . . ."

"I'm a grown ass man," Deacon replied. "I don't *have* to admit anything."

"But—"

"I have enough going on right now. I don't need you on my case, too," Deacon interjected. "So can we stop with the inquisition?" Deacon tugged at the white laces on his sneakers. "I swear, you're as bad as Kai."

The nine-year-old boy Miller mentored was famed for asking a million questions a minute. And not run of the mill fluff. Hard hitters that made a man question his every move.

Miller's mouth parted in offense, but he swallowed his words as he slumped back in the chair.

"Thank you," Deacon said.

Miller's thumbs twiddled for a moment before he spoke again. "It's annoying as hell, and I don't know how he knows what he does, but Kai is usually right in his assumptions."

"That doesn't mean you are."

"You're not saying I'm wrong, though."

"For the love of everything—" Deacon tossed his sneakers to the bottom of his locker. "I'm starting to understand how you get caught up in so many fights."

"I'm just trying to figure out what's going on with you and this *woman.*"

"Who knows . . ." Deacon's head wavered. "That's the problem. I don't know where she stands. I'm not even sure if she knows where she stands."

Deacon couldn't even begin to process what she might be thinking. Reagan's thoughts were too fluid and too quick for anyone else to keep up with her process.

Miller's face skewed. "She's not sure about *you*?"

"It's complicated." Deacon pulled black athletic pants over his shorts.

"Then uncomplicate it." Miller's hands dropped as he pulled a green water bottle from the ledge that lined the lower rim of their lockers. "That's what you would tell me to do."

"It's not that simple," Deacon said.

"With women it usually isn't." Miller's eyes widened with understanding as he tipped the water to his plump lips. "So what's her hang up?"

Deacon swallowed back the confession he wanted to give and found a middle ground that wouldn't leave Miller or Reagan swinging fists in his direction. "She doesn't want anyone to know we're together."

Miller cackled as his feet lowered to the ground. Noticing Deacon's somber face, his laughter halted. "Wait. Are you serious?"

"Why the hell would I joke about someone not wanting to go public with me? It's not exactly flattering information."

Deacon scooped his jersey from the locker's bottom and draped the mesh material over one of three wood hangers. The metal hook hit the rack with a thud.

"Because it's ridiculous," Miller spouted, rising to his six and a half foot loft. Skepticism shaded his face. "Unless . . ."

"No unless," Deacon replied, shoving Miller back down to his seat.

"Then it doesn't make sense. There's not a better guy out there than you. Is she blind? Or is it because she isn't and you're black and she's white? And her family is wicked conservative or something?"

"Her family is far from conservative," Deacon replied.

"So what then? She's buying into the stereotype that all athletes cheat?"

"She'd just afraid," Deacon said, his palm wrapping his plastic bottle. "You know how it is when you meet someone but you're not sure if you should risk it all and fall the long fall."

"It's not an easy move to make. I won't argue that." Miller's long arms reached into his locker and pulled out his black duffle. "But you deserve someone who wants to take that chance."

"I agree, but I'm not ready to give up on her yet."

Miller pulled a set of clean athletic gear from his bag. "Well, you better figure out a solution soon because the dating show is not going to help your cause."

Deacon's right brow lifted. "That's the part that's actually bothering me the most. She wants me to do it."

"That's a bad sign," Miller said, tugging athletic pants over his long legs. "She can't really want you if she's encouraging you to date other women."

"That's what I'm afraid of," Deacon said.

Chapter Ten

TWO weeks later, chatter from the front of the house echoed throughout the backstage holding area at The Murat Theatre. A thin television screen mounted to the concrete wall showed a full house awaiting the tug of the red velvet curtain, but the left wing surrounding Deacon was eerily empty.

Used to playing with a team, Deacon was unfamiliar with the nervous jitters that came from a solo venture. That is, of course, what he blamed for his twisted stomach and fidgety fingers. It had nothing to do with the fact that Reagan was going to be in the audience that evening. That this was his one chance to make her jealous. To make her see she wanted him regardless of the cost.

Finding success would require walking a very fine line. A string thinner than a tightrope. And while Deacon was known for his grace under pressure, the weight of this venture had him wobbling with unease. One misstep would end it all.

No more late night chats about visiting exhibits at the State Museum.

No more heated debates over which little bistro in Paris is actually the best.

No more security in knowing that the person he was with liked him for him and not his fame.

"You ready?" Breaking his isolation, Stella's voice popped over Deacon's broad shoulders.

The athlete's firm hands adjusted the microphone attached to his lapel and smoothed down his pewter suit coat. He wasn't ready for any of the events that were about to unfold with the dating game. Or what they might lead to in his personal life.

"If I say no, will it matter?"

"No," Stella said, "Like it or not, you're going to do the series to keep yourself and others out of trouble."

Deacon's face wrinkled with confusion. "I'm not in trouble."

"Yet," Stella clipped. The twenty-six-year-old's flared, black trousers swayed with her forward stroll. "But you're bound to get burned if you keep playing with fire. Worse yet, you're going to take your friend's house down in flames, too."

"Shit." Deacon's palms ran down his contorted face. "I can't believe Kate told you."

"Kate is no *chota.*" Stella's hand waved off Deacon's words. "I suspected and her vehement denial merely confirmed my belief."

"Then how did you know?" Deacon's brow quirked with question.

"Oh, please. You both disappear for more than a few minutes at the same time." Stella's arms folded over her crimson blouse. "Not to mention, the way you stare at each other, yet avoid speaking. It's a dead giveaway. The only reason Miller doesn't see it is because he doesn't want to."

"Actually," Deacon's eyes dropped as he rocked on his dress shoes. "I think he has suspicions."

Stella didn't flinch at the athlete's admission. "Me, too. That's why I picked you for the show."

"Because you don't want Reagan and I together?"

"Because I want stability for my friend. Miller is finally on a better path, and he needs all of our help to make sure he stays there." Stella smoothed her hands over Deacon's shoulders and straightened the knot at his neck. "There are going to be five lovely women vying for your attention. Give it to them. Get off this downhill road that will lead to nothing but disaster."

"But—"

"But nothing," Stella replied, tugging Deacon's tie until his face was level with hers. "It's done. Move on."

She said it as if it were the easiest thing in the world. Yet, the athlete had attempted to keep a healthy distance from Reagan for weeks, and he'd failed time and time again.

Deacon's lips pursed. "I don't know if I can."

"You're one of the smartest athletes I know. You'll figure it out." Stella released her grip and turned on her heel. "Follow me. I'll show you the way."

"Of course," Deacon mumbled as his dress shoes drug along the black wood planks.

Any person of sound mind knew it wasn't wise to disagree with Stella. Beyond that, it was pointless. If she wanted something to be. It was.

So now, Deacon not only had to convince Reagan that they belonged together, he had to convince Stella as well.

All while feigning interest in other women.

Deacon's fingers stroked his wrinkled forehead while his heart thumped like a bass drum. The whole situation had disaster written all over it.

An eerie hush fell over the crowd, and pulled Deacon's attention to the stage.

A cheesy, upbeat love song sprang from the speakers as video clips detailing Deacon's life began to jump across a large screen that lowered from rafters. Friends and family members described his likes and dislikes while pictures of his past faded in and out. His grandmother's admiration of his trustworthiness and honest nature twisted like a knife in his heart. Her pearly smile wouldn't be radiating if she knew the lie he'd been living.

At the conclusion of the video, the auditorium lights dimmed before rising again in a light pink shimmer. Shrouded in the warm glow was the event's host, Rin Yamada.

The popular channel 7 reporter was one of Stella's best friends, so there was no doubt in Deacon's mind how she'd secured such a high profile position.

Perched on a plush, gray chair, Rin's knees tilted toward the empty seat adjacent to her own. A violet dress popped off her beige skin while ruby lips framed the toothy smile that widened with the audience applause as her introduction concluded. She appeared genuinely excited for the evening's events, and Deacon felt guilty for not matching her enthusiasm. But how could the athlete get pumped up when he knew this was likely the moment that would mark the beginning of an end?

"Thank you all for being here." Rin's chipper voice echoed up to the intricate molding circumnavigating the ceiling in the lofty auditorium. "The Public Education Foundation welcomes you to the opening night of our eighth annual Single in the City series. This three week ride is going to be wild, so buckle up and get ready for a race where charm, beauty, and speed collide!"

She paused while another round of applause erupted. When the clapping subsided, she continued her greeting.

"We all know you're excited for the festivities to begin, so let's welcome this year's bachelor, starting guard for the Indianapolis Panthers, Deacon Bailey."

Rin's hand lifted as her bare arm opened to the wings of the stage. While he debated walking out the emergency exit posted not a hundred feet away, Deacon straightened his tie once more. The soft silk felt more like a noose than a fine accessory. Then again, his simple, uncomplicated life was ending, so perhaps the strangled feeling was appropriate.

Deacon sucked in a deep breath, and with a heave of pent up emotion, the athlete's nimble feet led him forward. His brown eyes tapered as he walked into the harsh spotlight that circled the chairs set center stage.

As Deacon lowered to his seat, he glanced up at the audience, but they blended into a blinding glow. Still, he greeted the viewers with a wave.

"You're too kind," he said, nodding toward the crowd as his voiced echoed through the loud speaker.

"Based on that video, it seems as if *you* are too kind, Mr. Bailey. Wasn't his grandma's story the sweetest?" Rin's hundred watt beam prompted the crowd to erupt in yet another applause.

Deacon winced at the earsplitting screams. The athlete was used to playing in front of a roaring mob, but the sensation was different when dressed to the nines in a designer suit instead of athletic apparel.

Plus, he was used to being cheered on for having an actual skill. For a positive contribution.

Here, Deacon wasn't doing anything other than deceiving innocent women, so the applause nicked at his conscience instead of lifting his morale.

Once the crowd settled, Rin began her inquiry. "So tell us Deacon, what are you looking for in a love match?"

A small rim of sweat beaded at his neckline, but Deacon forced a smile despite the growing heat. Two spotlights radiated the heat of a hundred suns. He wasn't looking for a love match. He'd found one.

At least, he thought so.

Not that he could share that information.

"Umm ... the usual," Deacon began, squinting as his eyes adjusted to the harsh lighting. "Someone who is kind, giving, intelligent."

Preferably packaged in a flight attendant with auburn hair, striking blue eyes, and legs for days.

"Any other noteworthy qualities?"

Typically, Deacon would have listed honesty and integrity, but he didn't feel like he was in a position to ask for those qualities when he was in the midst of a deceptive scheme.

"I want a partner that I can do life with," Deacon replied, rubbing his open palm over the silky cloth that covered his thigh. "I want to raise a family with my best friend. Travel the world. Make everyday life an adventure."

"Music to my ears," Rin said, "and to all the ladies in the audience this evening. Am I right?" The crowd's applause thundered once more. "What woman wouldn't want the same?"

Deacon's forced smile drooped. He could think of one who was hesitant to accept his offer of such.

"Speaking of ..." Rin segued. "Are you guys ready to meet the ladies vying for Deacon's heart?"

The crowd cheered with eagerness.

"That's what I thought," Rin announced. "Get ready, Deacon Bailey, because once you lay eyes on these beauties, your life is never going to be the same."

Chapter Eleven

"HOW is Deacon going to choose?" An enthusiastic Kai shouted over the clapping crowd. The whites of his eyes widened with delight. "All of these girls are super pretty."

"If he's into short skirts and overdone makeup." The lavender cotton of Reagan's fitted tee crumpled as she leaned into the armrest.

It wasn't that she was jealous. She wasn't. Reagan was embarrassed for the women who had so little self-worth that they felt they needed to put themselves on display.

Besides, always practical and down to earth, Deacon would be repulsed by the parade of fake eyelashes and immodest apparel.

Wouldn't he?

"The fourth one has on a long dress," Kai argued, pointing to the tan skinned woman on stage who sported the most modest attire of any contestant.

Not that most modest meant wholesome. It was simply less slutty.

"It only goes to her knees," Reagan snipped. "And that scoop neck doesn't hide her assets."

"Deacon is conservative, but he's not Amish," Miller replied. "Based on what I see, I think he'll be into one from this set."

"Finally," Kai replied, brushing down his navy, school polo. "He hasn't had a girlfriend for forever."

Miller smiled at the little boy who'd been assigned as his little brother a few years prior. "Looks like Deac is back in the game now."

Kai smashed a high five into Miller's open palm.

From the aisle seat in the tenth row, Reagan watched five contestants strut across the large stage. Their heights and skin colors varied, but they all had long tresses tumbling with barrel curls. The waves framed charming faces that brimmed with beaming smiles, and their excitement chewed at Reagan's anxiety.

It was apparent from their triumphant grins that the women thought they stood a chance at capturing Deacon's attention. But Reagan knew that couldn't be further from the truth. Deacon liked women who were real. Someone that had depth and more to offer than big boobs.

At least, Reagan thought he did. After all, her figure was more sporty than voluptuous.

"You two need to stop giving Deacon a hard time." Kate's hand gently slapped Miller's bicep as her gaze narrowed in Kai's direction. "I'm sure he's had a good reason for his solitude."

Miller leaned back and wrapped his arm around Kai's chair. "Only it turns out he hasn't been as alone as he led us to believe."

"What?" Kate's body propelled forward in her seat while Reagan started for her feet. Kate's hand snapped up and grabbed the sleeve of Reagan's denim jacket, tugging her back down.

Panicked heat coursed through Reagan's bulging veins. *What did Miller know?*

"What did he say?" Creases formed on Reagan's forehead as she pulled her arm from Kate's grasp. Her khaki covered thighs slid to the edge of the padded seat. "Did he say who? For how long?"

"Or how old she is? Where she works? Any other details?" Kate asked.

"Deac just mentioned that he's been casually seeing someone. No names or specifics," Miller replied, holding up open palms. "What's with the quiz?"

"Nothing." Both women echoed at the same time.

Reagan dug through her small clutch, though she wasn't sure what she was searching for. The composure she needed wouldn't be found inside, but at least the gesture gave her hands a momentary task while her brain processed Miller's proclamation.

"It doesn't seem like nothing."

Reagan continued to search for nothing, then pulled out a tube of strawberry flavored chapstick as if that were the item she'd been trying to locate. She layered a quick line of gloss for good measure.

"We're just surprised Deacon has been seeing someone," Kate said.

Reagan added, "He usually tells us stuff like that."

"Well, if it makes you feel any better, he didn't even tell me until a few days ago."

"I'm sure Deacon had his reasons for keeping it a secret," Kate said, patting Miller's muscled arm.

"Yeah, like she's a crazy—" Remembering Kai was with them Miller corrected the word tumbling from his lips. "Witch."

"You know I know what you're talking about, right?" Kai's brown eyes rolled toward the balcony. "I hear way worse when I come with you to practice."

Miller's gaze flashed to Kate as he nudged Kai. "I'm sure you're mistaken. The guys are on their best behavior when you're around."

"Oh, right."

Kai's lips lifted to a coy smile as if he were the one trying to wiggle out of trouble. Kate was surely concerned about his slip of the tongue, but Reagan could only focus on Miller's retelling of Deacon's vulgar description of her.

"Did Deacon really say that though?" Reagan questioned, zipping her bag. "That the woman he's seeing is a *witch?*"

She knew Deacon wasn't pleased with her desire to cut ties, but did he think that little of her?

"Not directly," Miller said, his forearm leaning to the wooden rest. "But it was implied."

"How so?" Reagan's fierce stare narrowed at her brother.

"You women are as nosy as reporters." Miller's fingers ran through his blond locks. "All I'm saying is that it's obvious this mystery woman's stringing him along."

Reagan's lips pursed. "Maybe she's being cautious."

"With Deacon?" Miller's light brow lifted. "He's the most quality person any of us know. What is there to be worried about with him?"

"Relationships are complicated," Kate cut in, her hand wrapping Miller's bicep. "Everyone has their own approach."

"Yeah, well they become more complicated when you encourage the person you're seeing to participate in a dating show." Miller unscrewed the top from his bottle of water and took a swig. "She didn't even try to stop him."

"Maybe it's a sign she trusts him," Reagan countered. "Or maybe she thinks it's what's best for him."

"He seemed to think it was a sign she didn't care, but I guess it doesn't matter now." Miller's hand opened to the glowing stage. "Look at these women. Deacon and his former flame are doomed."

"You don't know that," Kate said.

"Yes, I do. She won't trust him for long with this set." Miller's sly grin grew. "I bet she's jealous as hell right now. How could she not be?"

Reagan shifted her gaze to the bright stage where spiked heels lifted ten toned legs. One contestant wore a tea length dress that hit just above her knee, while the others were wrapped in tight dresses too short for sitting. Still, their slender bodies roosted on high stools behind Deacon.

Her Deacon.

Due to their position, he couldn't actually see the women, but that didn't ease Reagan's growing concern. Deacon would lay eyes on them eventually, and she couldn't help but wonder if Miller was right.

Would Deacon be enticed by their beauty?

Would he want one of them more than her?

And what if he did?

A week ago, Reagan thought she wanted to Deacon to move on, but now that he was on the brink of doing so, she wasn't so sure of her decision.

But how could she keep Deacon without risking everything she held dear?

Chapter Twelve

THOUGH the spotlights carried the fire of a hundred suns, Deacon was grateful for their intrusion. The blinding glow gave justification to his wretched face. He felt his skin crinkle further with each contestant's thoughtful response.

Seeing as they weren't Reagan, Deacon was sure he wouldn't be tempted by the women tossed in his direction. Yet, here he was, absorbing their answers with genuine curiosity.

He'd learned the blonde liked to cook and owned her own healthy meal prep delivery service.

Another worked as a yoga instructor who, on her days off, offered free classes for senior citizens at a local community center.

And the remaining three were just as accomplished.

Buying into the stereotype that only desperate sorts willingly participated in public antics such as the Single in the City series, Deacon assumed he would have to fake interest in the contestants.

But that wasn't turning out to be the case at all.

The women projected kindness. Intelligence. Savvy. And Deacon wasn't pretending to be intrigued.

Was that a sign that he was meant to move on?

Or was his mind simply craving the simplicity that would come with choosing one of the show's contestants?

"The votes are in," Rin announced, waving a pink envelope through the sweltering air. "Are you all excited to hear the final results?"

Cheers from the anxious crowd catapulted across the large auditorium. The rapping of hands caused Deacon's heart to pick up from its steady pace. Strangers were about to decide his fate for the next few hours. Maybe forever.

"First, we'll begin with the contestant leaving us this evening." Rin's lips dipped in a pout. "Sarah, I'm sorry. You've been voted out of the dating circuit. You won't be going on the group date this week."

Deacon's head tilted as his mouth drooped. Did the kindergarten teacher have to go? He'd admired her spirit and patience. Anyone who could manage two dozen, needy six year olds on a daily basis certainly had the giving nature he was looking for in a mate.

But alas, it appeared the universe had decided she was not for him. *Was anyone?*

Rin rose from her seat as the tall brunette ventured from her post to give the host a goodbye hug. Deacon lifted from his seat, assuming he was supposed to do the same. Her slender hip bumped his as they met in an awkward side embrace. Unsure of what to do, Deacon raised his hand in a high five. A puzzled look spread across her face, but the woman slapped the athlete's palm before she crossed the stage. A mixture of boos and clapping followed her departure.

The athlete wiped his beading brow. If their gawky encounter wasn't a widespread gif by morning, he planned to thank his lucky stars. For someone who was touted as graceful on the court, he lacked finesse on the stage.

Was it the crowd making him nervous? Or the women? Perhaps both?

Deacon was out of practice with dating, and he'd never cared for public arenas that weren't based around athletics. Though with the way his heart was pounding, the athlete felt as if he'd just sprinted a mile.

"Now, for the lucky winner of tonight's one on one dinner date with Deacon." Rin's extended pause let the crowd's excitement build.

Although a pleasant evening was likely to ensue with any of the contestants, Deacon sent up a silent prayer that the audience picked the woman named Saachi.

While all the women were interesting, there was an inexplicable intrigue haunting his mind when it came to the woman in the violet dress. At twenty-eight-years-old, she was established in her career, seemed settled in her own skin, and gave the impression she was there for the right reasons.

Also, Saachi claimed to prefer nineties music to the modern pop the other women claimed they adored. To Deacon, music of the past held more substance and meaning than mindless fluff that filled current contemporary radio stations.

Music alone couldn't determine a person's personality, but it gave Deacon hope that they'd find a few commonalities to discuss over dinner.

If Rin said her name.

As anticipation mounted, drum like music crescendoed in the background. After what seemed like minutes, Rin shouted, "Saachi."

With the host's announcement, the crowd erupted in applause, and Deacon's shoulders relaxed. Luck hadn't been on his side lately, so the athlete was relieved that at least a minor grace was thrown his direction.

"There's a driver out back waiting to whisk you two off," Rin said, hands swooping to call the contestant forward. "But first, Saachi come up here."

Long legs strode toward the host as the woman pushed gently curled, onyx hair behind her shoulders. Taking Saachi into view for the first time, Deacon admired how her purple, tea length dress perfectly accented her sandy skin while flushed cheeks highlighted her round face. Even under the harsh glow of stage lights she was striking. Certainly the type of woman Deacon would have been interested in before Reagan.

Deacon glanced to the invisible crowd.

What did Reagan think of their selection?

Was she jealous? Or was she as pleased as the roaring audience?

He hoped it was the first, but a nagging tug at his heart worried it was the latter.

Rising to his feet, Deacon strolled to meet Saachi mid stage. Her arms greeted him with a hug and a gentle kiss on the cheek. Turning to the audience, Deacon let his hand linger behind her back to which the audience voiced their approval.

A smile drew on Saachi's lips as hoots and hollers floated from all directions. Lifting from her slender frame, her small hand waved to the masses. Shoulders back, and her head held high, Saachi was poised despite the surrounding calamity. In fact, she didn't appear to mind the hubbub at all. She seemed satisfied to be the one on Deacon's arm.

That led Deacon to wonder, if a perfect stranger could be content by his side in public, why couldn't Reagan?

Chapter Thirteen

"S o . . ." Deacon's jittery hand pushed St. Elmo's famed shrimp cocktail appetizer to the center of the table as he forced a smile toward Saachi. "What do you do? For a living?"

It was a lame question, but the athlete hadn't been on a first date for quite some time. Plus, the last time he went out with a woman, he hadn't been surrounded by two cameramen and a glaring light, with a mic taping his every word.

Nor had he ever been on a date with the intention of staying in the friend zone. It was ironic, how it was more difficult to keep a date platonic than to try to seduce a woman. Shouldn't it be the other way around?

And if he wasn't trying to make a move, why was he so nervous?

"I own a boutique in downtown Zionsville," Saachi said, scooping two curled shrimp to her plate while faint jazz music floated between high tables in the bar area. "We carry on-trend women's clothing that ranges from casual to cocktail."

Unphased by the commotion surrounding their table, a soft smile graced her painted pink lips as her glittering lids lifted.

Where Reagan's eyes were light, Saachi's were dark. The rich color of fresh brewed coffee before it was diluted by creamer.

Deacon had transitioned away from that particular morning

indulgence years ago, seeing as coffee had too much caffeine and wasn't good for his game play. And Saachi's particular brand would be exceptionally bad for his relationship with Reagan.

"Very nice. What's your shop called?" Deacon asked, his stiff spine leaning toward the table in an attempt to shift the glare of the spotlight. "Maybe I've heard of it."

"Do you frequent ladies' boutiques?" Saachi's thin eyebrow lifted playfully.

"No. But my . . ." Deacon's voice trailed off because he couldn't note Reagan's fondness for clothes while being taped, nor could he mention why he had in depth knowledge of a woman's shopping habits. "My friends do. The women. Not my teammates." The athlete's sweaty hands wiped the cloth napkin on his lap as his gaze darted to the dating show's camera lens. "Not that there'd be anything wrong with it if they did, but it's just not who they are." Deacon's wrinkled face turned back to his date. "If you'd ever met them, you'd understand what I mean. They are kind of rough around the edges."

"It's okay. I get it." A chuckle erupted from Saachi's chest as she placed a calming hand on Deacon's forearm. "We all have friends like that."

Deacon's body shuddered at Saachi's soft touch.

What would Reagan think when she watched this episode? Would she be bothered by the gentle graze?

Or would she blow it off as unimportant? Knowing Reagan and her recent ramblings, she'd probably encourage Deacon to return the gesture.

Recoiling his arm, Deacon leaned to the leather padded back rest. "Yeah, but athletes are a unique breed. They're difficult to understand unless you really get to know them on a more personal level."

"Well, that's what I'm trying to do," Saachi reminded as she slipped a shrimp from the prongs of her fork. "Get to know you."

"Right," Deacon nodded as he took in the cameras, lights, and the staring crewmen. "Despite the craziness currently surrounding me, at the end of the day, I'm a pretty simple guy. A lot of professional athletes live fast paced lives, but that's not really my style."

"I read that about you," Saachi said, pulling a roll from the bread basket. She tore a small piece and lathered it with butter. "Not to be creepy, but I did a little online research once I learned you were the bachelor."

"It's a hazard of dating in the twenty first century," Deacon said with a shrug, reaching for a roll as well. His diet didn't allow for an abundance of white flour, but given the events of the last week, the athlete decided he'd earned the treat. "I'd rather talk about you, though. You never told me the name of your shop."

"Oh, right. My boutique is called House of Chennai as in—"
Deacon's eyes lifted. "The city, of course."

Though he didn't make it to Asia as often as he liked, Deacon was fascinated by eastern civilization. Their value of family and stream-lined living were both topics on which American's could take note.

"You're familiar with India?" Surprise highlighted Saachi's face as her fingers moved to the thin stem of her wine glass. Burgundy liquid swirled with the gentle sway of her hand. "My parents grew up there before they moved for my father's medical school training."

"I've been a few times," Deacon said, taking a swig from his beer. "I love the culture. The vibrancy. The sea. Though I'm always glad to come home to a good cheeseburger."

"Ah, yes. Beef. I do love a good steak." Saachi's upper body leaned toward Deacon as a wry smile lifted on her lips. "But don't tell my mother." Her head turned to the camera crew. "I really hope she isn't watching this."

Deacon's lips lifted as Saachi turned back to the table. "Your mom wouldn't approve, huh?"

Considering his mom was beyond supportive of his every move, it was hard for Deacon to consider what it might be like to have parents who disproved.

"She doesn't condone much of what I do," Saachi said with a sigh. "I'm too American for her taste. Though, I'm not sure how my parents expected my sister and I to become proper Indian women with all of the influences of western society knocking at our doors."

Deacon smirked. "Like beef?"

A smile formed on Saachi's lips as a flirtatious wink flashed from her lids. "More like men."

"Your mother doesn't want you to date?"

Deacon's face wrinkled as he pondered the oddity. Every time they gathered, the athlete's family hounded him about bringing home a significant other, so he couldn't imagine what it would be like to have a family that discouraged him from spending time with women.

The tablecloth scrunched under the push of Saachi's elbows as she leaned toward the athlete. "She'd prefer I skip that part of the process and just get married. To a man of her choosing."

A grimace formed on Deacon's face. "She wants to arrange your marriage?"

While Deacon loved his mother dearly, the thought of her picking his future wife was terrifying. Wanting someone to nurture her son, Ines Bailey would select a southern debutante type. A woman who was soft, demure, cooked like Rachel Ray, and wore pearls to the grocery store. And though all of that sounded nice in theory, Deacon was looking for something more in his forever.

He wanted substance. A challenge.

He didn't need a perfect woman. Just one who was perfect for him.

In acknowledgement of Deacon's disdain, Saachi's right shoulder lifted. "Arranged marriages are common practice in other parts of the world."

"I know." Deacon cleared his throat as he reached for a water glass. That didn't mean he had to agree with the practice. "But no one should be forced into something as serious as marriage. You should have desire, love, commonalities."

The things he shared with Reagan.

"I agree, but she doesn't see it that way. She thinks love can grow over time."

"What about you?"

"Arrangements work for a lot of people, but I've always held out hope for a love match. That's why I'm doing this show."

Deacon's face skewed with concern. "Because you think you could love me?"

A chuckle burst from Saachi's lips as her hand covered her lapel mic. "I don't know you well enough to know that. But by doing such a public show, I've completely ruined my reputation in the local Indian community. No parent will approve of me as a match for their son. They'll all think I'm a trollop."

"Yet you're smiling?" Deacon's mug lifted as his sipped the golden liquid.

Saachi nodded as her hand fell to her glass. Hope lit in the rims of her pupils. "Yeah. After this show is over, my real life begins again. I'll get to write my own future."

Deacon face dropped.

Saachi's positive outlook highlighted how glum his own had been in the last few days.

But how could he look on the bright side when things were spiraling downhill with Reagan? And what was he supposed to do to change their trajectory?

In theory, he could tell Miller the truth and see where the cards landed, but he didn't want to go behind Reagan's back to do it. He wanted her to want to tell the truth. Wanted her to want them. Him.

"Won't your family be disappointed?" Deacon asked.

"Oh, my mother will be mad for a few weeks, but she'll come around," Saachi said. "And my father won't bat an eye. He just wants me to be happy."

"I'm happy for you, too," Deacon said, his fork prongs pushing at his shrimp. "We all deserve the kind of future we dream of."

"Agreed," Saachi said. "So tell me, Deacon, what's your dream?"

Deacon's brown eyes faded to his creased, cloth napkin as his chest released a sigh. "It's complicated."

"Dreams worth having usually are." Focused on her date, Saachi sipped her wine. "But complicated doesn't mean impossible. If you're willing to put in the effort, anything can happen."

A clatter sounded as the athlete's utensil dropped to the ceramic plate. "If only that were true."

Saachi's head tilted with curiosity. "In what aspect of life is it not?"

"Relationships." Deacon's back slumped to the upholstered cushion. "Love."

"I see." Saachi pursed her lips as her hand fell to the athlete's arm. "There's a woman who got away?"

Deacon's head shook. "You can't lose someone you never really had."

"I disagree. Feelings, even when one sided, can be very real." Saachi's thumb brushed Deacon's cuff. "But I'm certain one day you will find the person you are meant to be with. As will I."

"Your optimism is admirable," Deacon said, covering her hand with his. "Your curtesy, as well. You're one of a kind to sit here and let me whine about another woman while we're on a date. This probably isn't how you expected this evening to go."

"I wasn't sure what to expect considering all of the stereotypes about professional athletes, but I find your realness to be a breath of fresh air." Saachi's lips turned up to a soft smile.

"Yours, too." Deacon replied.

And it wasn't a lie. It was refreshing to spend time with a woman who wasn't afraid to go against everyone in her world for a chance at happiness.

A woman who wasn't running away.

Chapter Fourteen

REAGAN'S eyes burned with irritation as she glared at the tablet resting atop her legs. She'd promised herself she wouldn't rush home and watch the live stream of Deacon's date. That she didn't care what happened with Saachi. But slouched on the couch, Reagan found herself rewinding the first episode for the fourth time.

Clicking the play button once more, the dinner scene unfolded. Her gaze focused on the corner of the screen where Saachi rested her hand on Deacon's arm. Reagan couldn't help noticing how Deacon didn't shutter or pull away from the stranger's touch. He'd allowed her possessive fingers to linger as if he wanted them there.

Did he want them there?

Or was he just being nice?

Deacon was well known for his kindness, but even he stood up for himself when physical boundaries were crossed.

And he wasn't standing.

Or shirking.

Or doing anything other than accepting Saachi's move.

Slamming the cover closed, Reagan chucked the tablet to the far end of the couch. She'd underestimated the prowess among the women in the competition. Upon first inspection, they'd all appeared vapid and senseless, but this one was surpassing expectations. Saachi was a secret seductress. Acting demure, when she was really a hellcat.

Could the temptress have shoved her chest up any further while she laughed? Her dress wasn't low cut, but it wasn't hiding her voluptuous figure. And the way she tilted her head and batted those long lashes. Saachi's intentions were more than clear. She didn't want freedom like Reagan. She wanted to be tied down . . . with Deacon.

Reagan's back sank further into the couch cushions as her arms folded across her slumped body. Deacon's date with Saachi wasn't even the worst of it.

Miller mentioned that Deacon was going to stop by tomorrow after his group date concluded.

Deacon would spend tomorrow afternoon surrounded by multiple beautiful women. Four, to be exact. Temptresses who would be throwing themselves at him, no less.

So what would Saachi do to further her pursuit and put herself ahead of the pack?

Hold Deacon's hand?

Aim to steal him away from the group for a quick kiss?

Reagan shuddered at the thought of Saachi's fishy lips touching Deacon.

Why had she ever thought the dating show was a good idea?

"That's not a good look," Kate said, strolling into the living room.

Miller had gone out with a few teammates following the live show, and the flight attendant was annoyed that her brother's girlfriend was even at his apartment in the first place. Even more peeved that she'd disrupted Reagan's skulking. But that was Kate. Always sticking her nose in other people's business.

"I can't dress down in my own house?" Reagan snipped, pulling a blanket over her yoga pants, hoping Kate would take the cue to exit.

"I meant the face," Kate replied, circling a finger around her own. "What caused such a scowl?"

"Nothing," Reagan snipped. "This is just my face."

"It's your face, lately. When you're upset with Deacon."

Reagan tucked the blanket around her frame and attempted to push the tension from her expression. "Why would I be upset with Deacon?"

"Oh, I don't know," Kate said, sinking to the coffee table in front of Reagan. "Maybe because he's out on a date with another woman."

"It's just dinner. And St. Elmo's is overrated." Reagan feigned indifference to the city's legendary restaurant.

"How do you know they're at St. Elmo's?" Kate quizzed. "Rin didn't announce that this evening."

Knowing she'd been caught spying, a hard swallow ran down Reagan's throat. "I *may* have watched part of the live steam."

"And you didn't like what you saw?" Kate's arms crossed.

Reagan's shoulders lifted with an unconvincing indifference.

Kate's head tilted. "You need to talk to him."

"I tried to the other night, but we circled back around to where we are."

"Why?"

"Because I don't want to hurt Miller like I did last time. When Brandon and I broke up, Miller lost his best friend and gained the worst reputation."

"He was the one who decided to deck the guy in the middle of a game," Kate argued. "That wasn't your fault."

"But I created the situation that led to the fight, and I won't do it again." Reagan's fingers fiddled with the fringe wrapping the edges of the blanket. "Miller has been so good to me over the years, forfeiting his high school fun to play basketball because he knew it could be our ticket to a better life. Paying for my college. Giving me a free place to live now, even though I disturb your alone time."

"Those aren't debts you have to repay," Kate said. "He isn't keeping a tally."

"But I am," Reagan said. "It's my turn to make the sacrifice. Deacon and I can't be more than friends, so I have to get used to it being less."

Kate nodded with understanding as her eyes scanned Reagan's casual state. "Then you're going to need to get ready to go out."

Reagan's forehead creased. "Why?"

"If you're hell bent on playing the martyr, you're going to need to come with me." Gripping the flight attendant's hands, Kate pulled her from the couch. "I was going to skip this week because Rin and Stella planned to go late, but it's the only way you'll survive this insanity."

Reagan didn't feel like venturing out in public, but the furrow in Kate's brow indicated she wasn't going to take no for an answer.

"Where are we going?" Reagan looked back as she headed for her room.

Grabbing her purse from the stand near the entryway, Kate tugged the strap over her shoulder. "It's Thursday."

NOTES FROM A MARIACHI TRUMPET flared across the local cantina where Reagan sipped tequila with Kate and her two best friends, Rin and Stella. It was no wonder their group was devout in their weekly gathering. The tacos were served on fresh made corn shells, the margaritas were strong and barely laced with mixer, and their favorite waiter, with his dark features, was more than easy on the eyes.

In response to one of Rin's quips, laughter spilled from Reagan's lips, but despite outward jubilation, a sadness tugged at her heart. Kate had only invited her to tag along because Deacon was dating other women. One of whom was Saachi. With her beauty, charm, and success, she was the kind of woman Reagan couldn't compete with even if she tried.

"Thanks for letting me join you guys this evening," Reagan said, her eyes scanning the genial gazes of the three other women in the booth as she stirred her third margarita. "I know you don't usually include outsiders, but I appreciate the distraction."

The wobbly table shook as Rin's elbows leaned into the tile top. "Count yourself as one of the gang. You're welcome to join any time. Especially considering..." Voice dropping off, Rin's black brows lifted as her hand opened to the group.

Reagan's face paled. "Considering what?"

Rin's brown pupils darted between Kate and Stella. "I mean, we all know, right?"

"Know what?" Reagan snipped.

"That you have a thing for Deacon," Rin replied, her brow wrinkling as she scanned her friends faces. "I thought this was common knowledge."

Reagan pivoted toward Kate as her eyes bugged. "You told them?"

"Of course, not," Kate hissed, her back straightening.

"There was nothing to tell," Stella said with the wave of her hand. "You two are so obvious, a blind man could have picked up on your little affair."

"You know, too?" Reagan's face fell to her palms. "*Shit.*"

"Why do you think I pushed Deacon to the dating series?" Stella whisked a long, mocha lock behind her shoulder. "Someone had to intervene before you two ruined all of my hard work."

"Miller is wary, but he hasn't completed the puzzle," Kate said to Stella.

"Yet," Stella snipped.

Kate continued, wrapping Reagan's arm with her hand. "Even if he did put it together, I think he'd take it better than you expect."

"Thinking and knowing are very different, and I don't take chances," Stella said, sipping from her glass.

Reagan huffed. "He's not going to find out because Deacon and I are going to keep our distance."

"Good," Stella said.

"You're so cynical." Rin's head shook. "What if they're meant to be together?"

"That's a storybook sentiment," Stella said. "There's always someone else waiting around the corner. You just have to venture that way to find them."

"She's right," Reagan said. "Deacon is moving on with the dating series, and eventually, I'll find some other distraction, too."

Rin sank back into the plush lining of the booth. "You're not going to fight for him? I would fight for Andrew."

"After five years, Dr. Carter is still procrastinating on a ring, so you very well may have to," Stella added.

"Residency is extremely time consuming," Rin argued. "He's just focused on his work right now. As he should be. But if it comes down to it, I'll do whatever it takes to keep him. Just like Reagan should do with Deacon."

"What's the point?" Reagan asked. "We haven't been together forever like you and Andrew. And every time we try to get together, something goes wrong."

"Like Miller getting arrested," Stella clipped.

Reagan rubbed her temples. "Exactly."

Stella added, "Which is why it's a good idea that you both pursue new interests."

Rin sank back into the plush lining of the booth as her gaze narrowed. "You're really sure you want to move on?"

Reagan's shoulders lifted. "There's no other choice."

"Well, there's always—" Rin began.

Stella's hand lifted as she cut in. A slight smile shaping on her lips. "She spoke her peace. Now onward we go."

"Let me guess, you have a plan?" Kate's head tilted.

"Always," Stella said, leaning into the table as her sharp eyes met Reagan's. "The best way to get over one man, is to get under another."

Chapter Fifteen

"**A**s you can see, I was gifted all of my abilities in athletics, not the arts." Deacon's paint brush stroked a blotchy maroon line across a ceramic dinner plate.

Five days after his solo date with Saachi, he and the four women remaining from the dating series were draped in white aprons as they decorated pottery pieces at The Creative Kiln. Thus far, the group date hadn't been as awkward as Deacon expected, but it hadn't lacked in random bumbling and oafish behaviors on his part. He'd never had Miller's charms, but he'd also never felt foolish around women. Then again, he'd never attempted to date while still pursuing another relationship.

Despite his clumsiness and lack of painting skill, the women still seemed interested in spending time with him. Not that Deacon was surprised. Women tended to overlook a lot to have a shot with a professional athlete.

Of course, they were unaware of the drawbacks of the gig. Like how frequent travel for games meant long stints of time apart. How holiday and birthday celebrations came second on the schedule. Not to mention, the jealousy that could ensue from knowing beautiful women are always attempting to lure your significant other away.

The kind of jealousy that he'd hoped would inspire Reagan to see their relationship in a different light. However, her blasé dismissal of the dating show left him wondering if the fiery redhead had a jealous bone in her body.

With a screech, Saachi scooched her chair a little closer to Deacon and leaned over his shoulder. Her dark strands swayed with her move, just barely brushing his pale blue polo. As she leaned in, her coconut essence pushed Deacon's mind toward the beach. It was fitting, he decided, seeing as hanging out with Saachi was turning out to be as easy as sunning with sand between the toes.

"What are you trying to make over here?"

Deacon's head wavered, his hands opening to the piece. "I don't even know. I'm lacking vision at the moment."

Dark streaks swirled in the water as his brush wound about the rinsing bowl. The athlete once considered himself a man with a plan. But in the last few weeks, everything seemed to be veering off course. Reagan wanted to part ways, Stella pushed him into the dating show, and now . . . Deacon glanced at Saachi.

Was she supposed to be part of the plan that lead him back on track?

Deacon couldn't figure out if Saachi was a solution or a problem.

"Feeling off kilter isn't surprising with all of this going on." Saachi's neck craned as she nodded toward the camera crew that hovered nearby. "It's throwing off your chakras."

"His what? Shock rocks?" The blonde named Caroline jumped in from across the table. Hilly curves of confusion lined her forehead. "Is that a basketball thing?"

"It's not sports related." Saachi's soft barrel curls rocked with the totter of her head. "It's a spiritual thing."

"You're familiar with chakras?" Deacon asked.

Could this woman be any more perfect?

Deacon turned to Saachi, taking in the true warmth of her mahogany eyes for the first time. Like stained wood, oaken streaks hovered near her pupils. The dark jewels were different from Reagan's ocean like pools. Not that Deacon was surprised. Saachi seemed the opposite of Reagan in every way. And not just in appearance.

Reagan was feisty and full of fire, where Saachi was calm and refreshing like water. Both key elements to sustaining life—but detrimental in excess.

Potentially deadly when handled incorrectly.

"I'm familiar enough with metaphysical concepts to know that it's no coincidence you chose green paint. And the placement of your strokes in the middle is telling as well." Saachi's finger pointed to the thick line down the center of the athlete's plate, her bicep brushing his as she moved.

Deacon was slightly discomforted by the fact that it didn't make him uncomfortable. "You're subconsciously trying to find balance in your heart," Saachi said, folding her hands in her lap.

"I'm pretty sure that would take more than this little bottle of paint to fix what I've got going on," Deacon said, swaying the plastic container between his fingers. "I'd need several gallons."

Even rearranging his apartment in accordance with the rules of feng shui several months prior hadn't proven successful in finding peace. So how was thin paint supposed to?

"Have you tried yoga?" Raven haired Ava asked. "I find it really centers me when I'm feeling out of sorts."

"I go at least once a week, but I can't seem to sweat out my troubles this time," Deacon said.

"Well, maybe you require communication rather than meditation," Saachi replied. "Reflection is good for personal processing, but it doesn't always lead to a resolution when others are involved."

"I hadn't thought of it that way," Ava said, pursing her lips.

The other women put on forced smiles as their eyes widened with interest. Assessing gazes darted from one to the other to Saachi.

Deacon wasn't surprised the other women were jealous. Saachi was worldly, yet humble. Outgoing, yet demure. The kind of woman who would turn any man's head. Any man who was looking for a mate.

Which Deacon wasn't. *Was he?*

No. He and Reagan had too much history.

Though she'd stated more than once that she was willing to toss their past to the side. Thought it was a good idea even.

So was it foolish to pass up a catch like Saachi for someone as uncommitted as Reagan?

Deacon glanced to the woman seated next to him. Was Stella's interference in his dating life a sign of how the universe wanted things to go? Had he been trying to force something that wasn't meant to be?

"I'm done with my vase," Saachi said, smiling up at Deacon as she draped her arms over his shoulder.

He tensed, remembering cameras were documenting their every move. "It's, uh, nice."

"Do you think they'd care if I started a second piece?" she asked, glancing to the far wall where a producer stood. "We're scheduled to be here for another hour, and although it wouldn't be miserable to sit here and stare at you, I figure I may as well paint while I compete for your attention."

"I say go for it. It's on me if they mind," Deacon said, waving to the shelves teeming with ceramic statues, plates, bowls, and ornaments in every shape and size before his gaze shifted to her.

"You're too sweet," Saachi said, her palm covering his hand as she slanted toward his ear. "And in case you're wondering, you'd have my attention, even if we weren't on a show."

Deacon's lashes blinked in rapid succession as he nodded in acknowledgement of Saachi's statement.

She made it so simple. Admitting her growing feelings. It was something Reagan hadn't been able to do in months after years of knowing him.

The remaining group continued to make pleasant conversation until their pieces were complete. When the three other women carried their work to the desk to be fired, Saachi's finger pushed her newest artwork toward Deacon.

"Here. For you."

"What is this?" Deacon's features wrinkled as he looked down to find a cerulean blue cow sitting on the canvas table covering.

"It's a cow," Saachi said, trapping her hands between her knees. Her smile radiated like the natural sunlight beaming in from the large window at the front of the shop.

"I see that." Deacon's head tilted toward his date. "But why did you paint me a cow?"

"Cows are thought to remove negative energy. I couldn't get you a real one, so I thought this would do." Saachi's nose crinkled. "Although, now that I think about it, maybe I should have just gone for a steak? They do say food is the way to a man's heart . . ."

"Nah, this is perfect." A grin lifted on Deacon's lips as he picked up the tiny statue. "Why blue though? Is it diseased?"

"This part of the color wheel is known for healing and removing pain," Saachi said, pushing a loose strand behind her ear. Her voice softened. "I don't know what you're going through, but I can tell something heavy is weighing on your shoulders, so I hope this will help settle that energy."

How could Saachi be so perceptive to Deacon's anguish and Reagan be so blind? She hadn't acknowledged his bruised feelings, yet the woman he'd known for mere days was trying to provide a comfort when she sensed a need.

"Thank you," Deacon said. "I can feel the difference already."

And he could.

His chest felt lighter and the tension in his temples was fading. Not because of the cow but because of what it represented.

Effort.

Deacon didn't have to concoct a scheme to gain Saachi's affection. She was giving it freely. And he liked it.

Chapter Sixteen

MINUTES passed like hours as Reagan waited for Tuesday evening to arrive. She scanned through television channels, attempted to read a book, painted her nails. But nothing drew her mind away from Deacon's day date.

Not showering.

Not curling her hair.

Not even the photo Stella had forwarded of her own escort that evening.

Okay, so perhaps the snapshot of the devilish fireman had caused her brain to take a moment's pause. He was, after all, one of the men selected for the annual Hearts on Fire calendar, and he wasn't wearing the top half of his uniform.

Plus, he had an eight pack.

And his dripping, blonde hair was tousled in a way that made a woman want to run her hands through it.

And his smile was aloof and charming as hell.

But he wasn't Deacon.

Deacon, who had been expected an hour prior to the six chimes that sounded from the courthouse clock.

So what was keeping him? Or rather, *who?*

Before the hands swung to seven, Reagan's waiting ears picked up a faint knock at the door. Jumping off the couch and sliding across the floor, her fingers coiled the silver knob and swung the barricade inward.

"Miller," Reagan called out to her brother in the other room. "Deacon is here."

Finally.

"I'm finishing this email to my agent. I'll be out in a sec," Miller replied from his home office.

As dashing as ever in his upscale casual polo and dark, fitted jeans that hugged his muscular thighs, Reagan's heart skipped a beat at the sight of Deacon. However, her fluttering core was soon calmed by the reminder that he'd dressed to impress someone else.

Several someone elses.

Including Saachi.

"You're late," Reagan said, forehead scrunching. "You're never late."

Deacon's eyes dropped to his platinum watch to double check her statement. "I also never date multiple women at once, but here we are."

Reagan's sandals trod back to give the athlete room to enter.

It was odd that he swished by without doing so much as a double take on her flowy tank and skin tight jeans. Deacon usually struggled to peel his eyes away from her fitted denim.

"I thought you were going to bail on Miller."

On her, as well.

"I debated it because I'm pretty tired," Deacon replied, yawning as he stepped inside. "It's been a long day."

"Oh, yeah?" Reagan's brow furrowed.

Long from what kind of activity?

"It's a lot," Deacon said. "Balancing time with the women. Trying to complete an activity while not making a fool of myself. Then, also trying to pay attention to what each woman is saying so I can respond appropriately." Deacon's toes nipped at his heels as he peeled off his brown loafers. "Superman couldn't do it and look suave."

"Why does it matter how you look?" Reagan inquired, swinging the door shut and leaning her back to the metal. "I mean, do you really care if you impress these women?"

"No, but I don't want to look like a fool in the videos. Image matters in my line of work, and the video stream has a wide reach," Deacon replied.

After years of watching Miller's reputation suffer for his actions, they'd all learned how much public perception could shape an athlete's life, so she couldn't blame Deacon for being wary.

Still, the notion that it might be more nagged at her thoughts.

Spotting a blue object snuggled in Deacon's palm, Reagan's brows perked. "What did you bring?"

"Uhh . . ." Deacon hesitated, tightening his grip as he whipped the object behind his back. "Just something I wanted to show Miller."

"What is it?" Reagan reached for the small item, but Deacon's body guarded the piece and angled away.

What was he hiding? And why didn't he want her to see it?

"It's not for you, so what does it matter?"

"I could ask you the same." Like a player on the court, Reagan's hands danced with Deacon's in a battle for the piece until he held it over his head where it was well out of her reach. "You shouldn't have brought something you didn't want me to see. This is my home, too, you know?"

"This was a gift for me, actually." The athlete pulled the ceramic piece back to his polo, his free hand stretching to block her approach.

"Oh, really?" Reagan's brow raised as her hand met her hip. "From?"

Not Saachi. Not Saachi.

Deacon's swift socks wound around Reagan's imposing form and looped for the kitchen. "Saachi."

"Of course," Reagan replied, following Deacon's path across the wood floor. Sarcasm oozed from her voice as she draped her legs across a barstool. "How kind of her."

"I found it thoughtful," Deacon snipped, placing the ceramic piece on the edge of the island where its beady black eyes stared Reagan down. "She noticed I seemed down, so she gave me the cow as a way to lift my spirits."

"Because she wants to lift other parts of you, too," Reagan scoffed, her pupils rolling to Deacon's groin.

Wouldn't it be her luck for Saachi to run more bases with Deacon in a week than Reagan had managed in months?

"Saachi isn't like that." Deacon's palms flattened against the marbled countertop as he slid between Reagan's thighs. "She's just being friendly."

"I was *just* your friend once, too." Reagan's elbows met the cool granite as she leaned back to meet Deacon's unflappable stare. "And look how that turned out."

Deacon's head dipped closer. "According to you it hasn't turned into anything."

"Deac." Miller's voice called from the back of the apartment. "Will you come read this email before I send it? You're better at commas and shit."

Reagan's pointer finger flipped toward the bedrooms. "Because the universe keeps doing that."

Not to mention, men were always changing their minds.

Even perfect Deacon could be swayed by a short skirt and a pretty face. Saachi was proof of that.

Proof that Reagan was right to hold on to her heart.

A burdened breath streamed from Deacon's lips as his chin rolled to his chest. "Life isn't fair."

"Maybe it is and we just don't realize it yet," Reagan said. "Maybe someday it will make sense why we couldn't be together."

Deacon's head wavered. "And maybe someday you'll realize telling your brother the truth isn't all that bad."

"Not likely," Reagan said.

She couldn't take that kind of chance on Deacon when his feelings were so easily influenced. He'd proven he couldn't handle conquering pressure when they'd first crossed the line at the hotel. His exit had been swift, without so much a backwards glance.

And she couldn't forget that.

Not when Miller had so much to lose.

"My thoughts exactly," Deacon said, pushing off the counter just as a knock on the front door echoed across the apartment.

Deacon's eyes scanned to the door and then back to Reagan, dragging the length of her body as if he'd just noticed her dolled up state.

The athlete's brow lifted. "Expecting company?"

"No," Reagan replied, making her way to the exit. "I'm going out."

Wrapping his arm gently around Reagan's waist, Deacon slowed her pursuit. His eyes narrowed as his voice tensed. "Out with friends?"

"Does it matter?" Shirking his grasp, Reagan pulled away. "It would be hypocritical of you to say yes considering you just went on a date with multiple women at once."

Deacon stepped in front of the door before Reagan's fingers could grasp the handle. "That's different."

"How?"

Deacon's hands pulled to his chest. "Stella set that up. Not me."

"Well, Stella set this up, too," Reagan said, shrugging off Deacon's concern. "So I guess we're even."

The flight attendant nudged Deacon to the side as she swung open the door. Her traitorous skin tingled at the touch, but she ignored the sensation.

"Hey. I'm Chase." The handsome stranger's face lit with a swaggering smile. "You Reagan?"

"Yup." Reagan returned his grin.

Chase peered at Deacon's leering shadow before flipping his gaze back to his date. "Are you ready to go?"

"Yeah, just let me grab my purse," Reagan reached for the coat rack where her bag was hanging.

As she did, Deacon peeked around the white frame. His eyes doubled when he saw who was standing on the other side.

Reagan's beam grew with his shudder.

She wasn't over Deacon, but that wasn't the point of the evening's outing.

It was to make Deacon think she was over him.

Because if he believed it, maybe she could, too.

Chapter Seventeen

AFTER Reagan made a swift exit, Deacon stormed back to Miller's office. He found the basketballer hovered over the keyboard, his eyes squinting at the glowing desktop screen.

"Do you know who your sister just left with?" Deacon growled, arms flailing toward the door.

"No." Miller's head shook as he looked up from the computer. "She said Stella was setting her up with someone, and with her insane standards, I just assumed it was fine."

"Since when don't you care who she spends time with?" Deacon asked, doing his very best to sound like a protective big brother rather than a jealous fool.

Miller's shoulders raised. "Kate's been on me to leave Reagan to her own devices when it comes to dating, so I'm trying to give her some space."

"Well, you picked the wrong time for that because she just left here with *Chase Howard.*" Deacon plopped down in the padded chair posted in front of Miller's desk. When Miller didn't respond, the athlete pressed the power button on the screen, forcing his friend to look up. "Chase *freaking* Howard. Indy Fire. Station Thirteen. Hangs with that cocky crew that's always at Lockerbie's."

Miller held up a palm to stop Deacon's rambling as he leaned back in his chair. "I know who he is. He used to hit on Stella all of the time back when we were dating, and it drove me nuts."

"But you don't care that he just picked up your little sister?"

"He's arrogant, but as far as I know, he's a decent person," Miller said, wrapping his hands behind his head as he kicked his feet up on the desk. "Besides, it's Reagan. She'll tire of him in a month or two, just like she did with the mystery guy she was seeing for a while. I haven't heard a thing about him in weeks."

Deacon folded forward in his seat and let his arms rest on his thighs. "You don't think she's into that guy anymore?"

"Of course, not," Miller said. "Reagan doesn't do commitment."

Deacon's lips sank.

How many times would he have to hear those words before his heart got the message and believed them?

Chapter Eighteen

TWO nights later, positioning a three point shot perpendicular to the goal, Deacon double bounced the ball before sending it soaring through the air. Sinking with a swish, the ball fell through the net, ending Deacon's perfect warm up. He hadn't missed a shot the entire pre-game practice session, and his fingers seemed to be on fire, sending ball after ball directly into the center of the hoop.

It was amazing. How good his game prep was going.

If only his personal life could flow so smooth. But that didn't seem to be in the cards for Deacon.

Though Reagan gave off a jealous vibe when he flashed his gift from Saachi, she hadn't given any indication that she wished to recant her statement about the pair moving on.

Not to mention, her recent date with Chase Howard, firefighting, womanizer extraordinaire, further pointed to her acceptance of their separate fates.

And to make matters worse, the universe seemed to be working against Deacon in every way. Cutting them off and pushing them apart.

So much so, that Deacon had to wonder if Reagan was right. Would they look back one day and see that splitting was all for the best?

"Way to go!" A familiar voice sounded over the rumbling crowd.

Deacon scanned the floor to find Saachi and a blonde, female companion filing into the front row on the opposite side of the court. She sported a Panther's jersey, with only a white sports bra underneath. The mesh fabric fit tight against her thin frame, and Deacon couldn't help but notice how the hunter green accentuated the excitement in her dark eyes.

Yet another complication he wasn't sure how to approach.

Saachi's fingers danced in a wave as her faded denim sank into the seat. The best in the house, per the athlete's request to Stella. Her first professional basketball game deserved nothing less.

Tugging at the back of his jersey, Deacon's raised brow prompted Saachi to curve and reveal her own. Heeding his call, she turned toward the crowded section and flashed a thumbs up. Seeing his number, the athlete sent a wink soaring her direction.

It was nice to see a woman he cared for, other than his mother, in his jersey. Being a Cassidy herself, Reagan always donned Miller's name and number. Deacon didn't mind, per se. After all, she was his sister. But there was something to be said for Saachi's public display of friendly affection, even if it was a small gesture.

"Are you going to stand there waving like an idiot? Or are you going to go say hi?"

Miller attempted to bounce a ball off Deacon's chest, but the athlete instinctively wrapped the sphere with his arms.

"Eh, I don't know if that's a good idea."

"Why not? We've still got four minutes left in warm up." Miller gestured to the scoreboard hovering over the center of the court. "You have plenty of time."

Deacon's eyes darted up toward the family suite. She was a small speck in the crowded loft, but Reagan's auburn hair popped from the dull brunette and blonde shades of the gathered mass.

While he wanted Reagan to feel the pangs of jealousy, Deacon had to find the balance between inciting envy and sparking rage. And considering Saachi was already a sore topic, Deacon wasn't sure it was wise to chat her up in front of a stadium full of fans while Reagan was within viewing range. Doing so was sure to hurt his cause.

Not to mention, the dating series producers weren't likely to appreciate Deacon showing favoritism to a contestant. At least, not at a time when they didn't have cameras rolling.

"I don't want to draw extra attention to them," Deacon mumbled, twirling a ball in his hands. "The show doesn't forbid conversing outside of taped dates, but it's frowned upon."

"So she's a rule breaker?" Miller replied, snapping his fingers to call a ball from one of the courtside assistants. "I like that about her."

Deacon's lips pursed. "You would find that to be an appealing quality."

"What?" Miller scoffed. "You need someone to loosen you up a bit."

The athlete took aim for his shot and sent the ball flying for the hoop. Bouncing off the backboard, the ball fell through the net. Miller's gaze moved from the goal to his friend. "You've always paved your own path and been more reserved, but the last few weeks have been a whole new level of weird, even for you."

"I'm just trying to take things slow and figure out what I want in life," Deacon replied, using his hands to wipe the bottom of his sneakers. "That's all."

"You're not taking it slow. You're not taking it anywhere," Miller argued.

Deacon's hands met his hips. "So?"

"It doesn't make sense," Miller said. "Saachi is gorgeous. She's into your weird karma stuff. She's successful. Yet, you're not trying to put any moves on her at all. Have you even *kissed* her?"

Deacon's cheeks flushed a darker shade of brown as he gritted his teeth. "No."

"Why the hell not?" Miller bellowed.

"I won't apologize for respecting women," Deacon snipped.

"I'm not saying you should force yourself on her," Miller replied. "But you've been on several dates, so I don't think a kiss is out of line."

"The timing hasn't been right," Deacon argued. "Not with the cameras and the other women. Having a game scroll across a thousand screens is one thing. A kiss is another."

"When you're really into someone you don't care who is watching." Miller's tilted stare moved from Deacon up to the family suite. "Unless you do care who sees . . ."

Deacon's heart raced faster than a horse galloping for the finish line. Miller voicing his suspicion was more than problematic. Deacon couldn't admit his relationship with Reagan until he knew with certainty what he was admitting to. He and Reagan needed to clarify where they stood before they put Miller on a whirlwind ride of emotions.

"Don't read into it," Deacon said, flipping Miller's ball from his grasp.

"It's hard not to." Miller's fingers combed his blonde pompadour. "I mean, it can't be . . . but it feels like—"

"Let it go," Deacon growled, tossing another shot to the net. "Nothing good ever comes from assumptions."

Deacon had to move his friend's mind off his current track of thought before he started to connect the dots. Which meant he was going to have to show interest in Saachi. Not that he wasn't interested in her. He was. But now he was going to have to show Miller which would risk Reagan seeing the same display.

Miller shrugged. "You know I can't stay away from trouble."

Apparently, neither could Deacon.

Chapter Nineteen

STROLLING out of the locker room after the game, Deacon draped his duffle strap from his shoulder. Concrete block walls reverberated the chatter of family and fans gathered outside, but Miller's voice sounded above the rest and drew his attention to the side.

"Mason, my man." Miller's palm opened to accept a high five from a little boy with curly hair. "I didn't know you were going to be here tonight. Did you graduate from home recovery?"

Miller had taken an interest in the boy after he started volunteering at the Donor Foundation with Kate. Mason's previous heart condition led him to a several month stint in the children's hospital, but eventually an organ donor came through. Now, the soon to be seven-year-old was well on his way to a more normal childhood.

A surgical mask concealed Mason's smile, but the gleam in his brown eyes radiated sheer joy. "Yup, so Kate got us tickets to celebrate."

"Good ones, I hope," Miller said with a wink as he sank to the boy's level.

The boy's head shook. "First row in the stands."

"We owe Kate a big thanks," Mason's mother chimed in. "Her friend, Stella, too. She set it up so we could come back here and meet a few of the players."

"Well, then, let's go for a tour," Miller said, nodding toward the locker room.

"We appreciate the offer, but Kate and her friend said that they were going to your usual after party, so we don't want to keep you from that. Besides, it's way past Mason's bedtime, and tomorrow is a school day, so we have to be going. But he insisted we wait until we saw you."

Miller motioned him closer as he lifted to his full form. "At least let Deac autograph something before you go."

"If you don't mind, that would be great." Mason's mother reached into her purse, pulled out a colorful rectangle, and handed it to Deacon. "Here's one of our tickets."

"It's no problem at all."

Deacon never minded signing memorabilia. Scratching his name was a small task, and it always spread joy to the recipient.

The athlete's hand dipped into his pocket, but remerged empty. "Do you have a pen or marker?"

Mason's mom fiddled through her bag, but her face wrinkled with dismay. "I usually carry one, but I can't find it."

"Here." A familiar feminine voice chimed in. "I always carry one."

Deacon's head turned to find Saachi standing by his side, black pen dangling from her fingers.

"Saachi?"

"Why do you look like you've seen a ghost?" Saachi's brow wrinkled. "You saw me on the sidelines. You knew I was here."

"Yeah, at the game," Deacon said, grabbing the pen and scrawling his name across the white back of the ticket before handing it back to Mason's mom. "But I didn't know you were back *here* here. How did you manage it anyways?"

Saachi's head tilted. "Your friend Stella invited me back so I could see you. We haven't really had any true alone time, so I thought it might be nice to have a moment to talk off camera."

Stella. Of course. She was always stacking the deck to play the cards she wanted, so Deacon should have known she'd do everything in her power to push him toward anyone who wasn't Reagan.

"That's why I know you." Mason's mother's eyes lit with delight as she peered at Saachi. "You're one of the contestants on Deacon's show."

"Ah, yes," Saachi said. "But if you could keep this little rendezvous a secret, I'd really appreciate it."

"It's not against the rules for us to be together," Deacon added for good measure. "Just frowned upon."

"Of course. My lips are sealed," the woman replied, pretending to zip her lips. "I do have to say though, I think you two would make a great couple."

"That's so sweet of you," Saachi said, smiling at the woman before shifting her gaze to Deacon. "We do get along rather well."

Deacon nodded in agreement. With their shared interest, conversations flowed easily and rarely held an awkward pause. More than that, Deacon enjoyed Saachi's calming presence. Rather than riling him up like Reagan, she grounded his emotions.

"We'll let you guys get to your celebration," Mason's mom said, pushing her purse strap higher on her shoulder. "But thank you for a wonderful night. We had a great time, didn't we, Mase?"

"Yeah, thanks," the little boy chimed.

"Anytime," Miller replied, accepting a low five from Mason. "And next game we're doing a full behind the scenes tour."

The young boy's eyes glittered with excitement. "Can I play on the court, too?"

Miller's fingers swooped through his blonde strands. "I think a full tour could include a little court action."

"Yes!" Mason exclaimed as an excited fist pumped into the air. "Will the rest of the team play with us?"

"Ok," Mason's mother interjected resting her hand over his curls. "I think we've made enough requests for one evening."

"But—"

"No buts. Time to go."

The little boy's shoulders sank. "Fine."

"Thanks again," the woman said, pushing her son along the concrete corridor.

"Bye," Mason drawled as he conceded to his mother's urging.

"Bye." Miller and Deacon waved to the duo as they strode away.

"I would have expected this from Deacon, but who knew?" Saachi began, a grin growing on her lips. "Big, bad Miller Cassidy has a soft spot for children."

"Spread the word." Heels clicked against concrete as Stella's alto voice broke into the conversation. "It's taken years of hard work to moderate his image, and we still have a ways to go before we're through with his reformation."

"Not that far," Miller scoffed.

"But how nice that you have someone to help you," Saachi said, turning her gaze to Deacon. "Everyone deserves to have someone who believes in them."

Deacon's lids lowered to the ground as his tennis shoe scraped against the concrete. Over the years, Reagan had supported him without fail. She'd been his cheerleader, his go to for advice and laughter. But given Reagan's recent date with Chase, the athlete couldn't help but wonder if she still cared for him in the same way.

Was their outing a ruse to make him believe she was moving on? Or was Reagan taking the suggestion she'd put forth several times and moving on?

"You wouldn't know it now, but Miller was almost a lost cause." Stella's hand met the red fabric of her sheath dress. "Lucky for him, I never give up until I get my way."

"I've heard that you're very dedicated to your job," Saachi said, cinching her leather clutch with both hands.

Dedicated was an understatement. Stella was ruthless when it came to her success.

And while that was fortunate for his best friend, Stella's tenacity was disastrous for Deacon since they wanted opposite results.

"I'm certainly steadfast," Stella said, her dark eyes widening with an idea. "But I do like to relax every now and again. Especially following a fifteen hour day."

Recognizing her play against him, Deacon's teeth ground. "It's getting pretty late, so we should all probably head home."

"Home?" Confusion spread on Miller's face.

"Of course, we *should* go home," Stella replied. "But we usually hit Lockerbie's after a game," Stella sent a smile soaring at Saachi. "You should join us."

Saachi's teeth tugged at her lower lip. "I don't know. I'm already pushing the limits of the show by being here, and I don't want interfere."

"Don't be silly," Stella said, swatting at Deacon's chest with a playfulness her sharp tone didn't convey. "Deacon, tell her she should come."

"Uhh . . . but won't people start making assumptions if they see us together in public?"

"She'll blend with the crowd." Stella waved off Deacon's concern as she turned to Saachi. "No one will even notice you're there."

There was truth to Stella's words. Regular patrons at the hole in the wall were used to the athletes in attendance and hardly paid them any attention. However, there was one person who wouldn't miss Saachi's presence.

Reagan.

Chapter Twenty

"YOU haven't said much this evening." Kate slid a vodka water adorned with two limes in Reagan's direction.

"What is there to say?"

Ice clinked against the low tumbler as Reagan's circled the cocktail straw as they waited for Miller and the other Panthers to arrive at their standard post-game gathering.

"I'm guessing you noticed—"

"That Saachi was sitting courtside," Reagan scoffed. "Yeah. It was kind of hard to miss with all the people trying to take pictures with her like she's some kind of *actual* celebrity."

"Thought you weren't the jealous type?" Kate sipped from the red straw poking out of her vodka cranberry.

"I'm not." Reagan's auburn tresses waved with the shake of her head. "But you may have been right in saying I was naive to think that it would be easy to move on. Deacon and I have too much history for it to be simple."

"I didn't want to be right," Kate said, wrapping Reagan's arm. "I hope you know that."

"It's not your fault," Reagan said. "I'm the one who drove him into the arms of his perfect match."

"Maybe he's going for her because he thinks that's what you want.

Maybe if you tell him how you feel, things could be different."

"What could be different?" Miller popped a kiss on Kate's cheek as he bent the straw and took a sip of her drink. His face wrinkled with displeasure as he placed the glass back on the counter. "That's disgusting."

"It's Tito's and cranberry juice," Kate said.

"Good liquor ruined by syrupy sugar," Miller replied, flagging down the bartender. "Can I get three buckets on my tab?"

The bartender nodded, shoveling ice into the tin containers.

"Three?" Reagan's brow wrinkled. "We always order two buckets."

"We have an extra guest tonight," Miller said, nodding to the Panther's usual table tucked in the corner.

"Since when do we invite outsiders to join the party?" Reagan questioned, folding her arms.

She didn't feel like mingling with strangers this evening.

"Chill. It's just Deacon's new love interest. We bumped into her after the game and invited her to join us." Miller threw three twenties on the bar and backed away with the buckets in hand. "You two should come meet her. She seems cool."

Reagan's head snapped to find Saachi clutching Deacon's arm, giggling over his shoulder like a lovesick high schooler. His head tossed back, joining in the laughter. A familiar gleam radiating from his dark eyes.

Kate's jaw went slack. "I can't believe he brought her here. He's—"

"Making it clear that he's moving on," Reagan finished, tearing her clutch from the counter. "I have to get out of here."

DEACON'S STOOL SCREECHED against the wood floor as he watched Reagan leave Kate's side and bolt for the hallway that led to the side exit. He suspected she wouldn't take Saachi's presence lightly, but he didn't anticipate her running out the door toward a dark alley minutes after their arrival.

"I'll be right back."

Prior to Miller's near catch a few months prior, the narrow corridor had been their meeting spot to share a few celebratory words and steal a few secret kisses.

And, on occasion, more.

However, with the wretched look on her face, the athlete didn't anticipate this session going that route.

Darting around post game revelers, the athlete's tennis shoes paced across the darkened bar. His hand wrapped the latched bar seconds before Reagan was able to push outside.

"What are you doing?"

"Leaving," she hissed.

The athlete didn't bother to ask why. There was no doubt in his mind that Reagan was upset by Saachi's presence. Still, she couldn't throw caution to the wind just because she was frustrated.

"You're not seriously trying to sneak into the alley by yourself at this time of night," Deacon scoffed, blocking the exit. "It's dangerous."

The Cassidy clan's lack of fear was going to do them all in one of these days.

Blue eyes glaring with glints of anger, Reagan attempted to push the athlete to the side. "You're not my keeper, Deacon. I can do as I please."

"Yeah. You've made that pretty clear." Deacon's feet held his stance.

As if he didn't get that memo when he watched her saunter away with Chase Howard the other day.

Chase *freaking* Howard.

"Why are you trying to stop me? I don't want to be here anymore."

"I'm trying to protect you," Deacon said, reaching for her hand, he brushed her knuckles with his thumb. "I care about you."

Snatching her hand away in a flash, Reagan smirked, "Oh, that's rich. Laughable really."

Anger boiled in Deacon's chest. He was trying to express his concern for her wellbeing, and she was laughing. "Can you take my affection seriously for one minute?"

"Not when you pretend to care about me while you're flirting with another woman right in front of my face." Reagan turned on her heel and stormed down the hallway.

"You went out with Chase." Deacon followed her hasty move, half yelling over her shoulder. "And I'm just playing the part that you told me to play because Miller was getting suspicious before the game."

Reagan skidded to a stop at the brink of the open bar area. Her cheeks flushed with anger. "Your acting skills are top notch. Perhaps you should consider taking on a movie role for the off season."

"As if I have time to be in your show and another one," Deacon snipped, leaning into the wood paneling. "Trying to be with you is a full time production these days."

Reagan stepped closer, and Deacon could smell vodka laced in her breath. "No one is forcing you to live this life. You can walk away at any time."

"As if I'll have the choice," Deacon replied.

"What does that mean?" Reagan's body stiffened as she took a step back.

Deacon's arms folded across his wrinkled tee. "You're so afraid of having something real, that I'm sure you'll run away before I get the chance to decide what I want."

Reagan's jaw clenched as she closed the space between them. "If I leave, it's because you're pushing me away."

Deacon's arms reached out and circled her back. Hauling Reagan flush with his body, Deacon crashed his lips into hers.

Caught off guard, her mouth went motionless for a moment, but she soon returned his affection. Reagan's warm palms wrapped his neck as she lifted to her toes, her hypnotic lips sending him into a daze. A trance Deacon wished he could live in forever.

If only Reagan would allow it.

Harsh coughing echoed down the long corridor, indicating they were no longer alone.

Dragging his mouth away, the athlete held Reagan's glassy gaze. Drawing up to his full height, Deacon's thumb ran over his lower lip. "Does that seem like pushing?"

Reagan's lashes fluttered a double beat. "I—"

"It *seems* irresponsible." Stella interjected, swatting her leather clutch at Deacon's arm she continued her tirade. "Haven't you two learned your lesson about public displays? And in the exact same place, no less. With Miller fifty feet away. I swear."

He wasn't mad that they'd kissed, but the athlete hadn't tailed Reagan with the intention of ravishing her in the hallway.

Not that he didn't want to.

He most certainly did.

The athlete found it hard to be in the same space and keep his hands to himself. But that wasn't why he followed her.

Deacon lifted his hands to block Stella's blows. "It was just a heat of the moment thing. We didn't plan it."

Embarrassed they'd been caught yet again, Reagan's cheeks flushed with the redness of a stoplight.

"Well, consider this your cool off." Stella's pointed finger waggled between them. "This is done. No more. Do you hear me? Done. Finito."

Glancing at each other, Reagan and Deacon both nodded their understanding.

"Don't let me catch you again," Stella snipped, waving them off as she strutted toward the restroom. "Or else."

Once Stella's heels clicked through the doorway, Reagan turned to Deacon, her hand massaging the back of her neck. "What do you think 'or else' is?"

Lips pursing, Deacon replied, "With Stella, it's hard to say. But I'm sure it wouldn't be pleasant."

The athlete had never experienced Stella's revenge to know the depths of hell she could send a man plummeting to, and he hoped to never be on the receiving end of her wrath.

However, when it came to Reagan, Deacon wasn't good with limitations, so the possibility of Stella having to exact her threat existed.

And they both knew it.

A slow sigh released from Reagan's lips. "At least she won't tell Miller."

Deacon's shoulders dropped.

Why was everything always about Miller?

With Stella.

With Reagan.

Couldn't anything ever be about *anyone* else? Deacon wasn't a selfish man, but was it so wrong to want to be more important one time?

And no one even knew with certainty that Miller would care if he and Reagan dated. Sure, things had gone wrong the last time Reagan hooked up one of his friends. But that was a different time with a different man.

Deacon fancied himself mature enough to maintain a friendship even if things went wrong with said friend's sister. But why was he the only one that could imagine that scenario?

Or was that what terrified Reagan?

That Miller might not mind.

"Right." Deacon's tennis shoe scraped at the wood floor. "Because if your brother found out, he might give his approval, and then you'd lose your reason not to commit."

Reagan's mouth twitched. "It's the twenty first century, Deacon. I don't have to be labeled a girlfriend or a wife to be happy."

"No, you don't. But you shouldn't tag them as horrible titles just because you're afraid." Deacon pushed a stray lock of hair behind her ear, his fingers lingering at her neck. "Not everyone is like your parents. There are people who have successful relationships and marriages."

Couples who weathered the storm. Who loved with their whole heart. Who supported. Who didn't run away at the first sign of trouble.

Why couldn't she see them?

Reagan shrugged away from his touch. "You're involved in quite a few *relationships* right now, so I suppose you would know."

The flight attendant tried to dart around Deacon, but quick on his feet, the athlete blocked her move to exit the dim corridor.

"Maybe so, but at least I'm putting myself out there. You don't even have close friends because you're so damn afraid of letting people in."

"I'm not afraid," Reagan replied, arms crossing over her chest as she turned for the alley exit.

"Then give me a chance to show you it could be different for us," Deacon called.

"Only fools take the same chance and expect different results." Reagan's head shook as she moved down the hall.

"But we're not those people. We change the equation."

Pausing at the exit, Reagan glanced back at Deacon. "And what if we don't? What happens if we're exactly the same as every couple who has failed?"

"I don't know." Deacon's lips pursed.

"And I do," Reagan said, cracking the door and allowing cool air to whip about the small space. "When we both stop chasing the wrong thing, the right thing will catch us, and then you'll see that I was correct."

"But—"

As if she didn't hear his plea, Reagan shoved into the alley and slipped from his sight.

Deacon's heart sank with the casual dismissal, but for the first time in months, he didn't pursue her.

Until she wanted to be caught, chasing Reagan was a fruitless endeavor.

He was certain that one day, she would learn she was so very wrong in her assumptions about relationships. But by then, it would be too late.

Deacon was tired of waiting. Tired of putting himself on the backburner.

Reagan had told him to move on time and time again.

So now, that's all that was left to do.

Chapter Twenty-one

TWO nights later, Reagan's eyes narrowed as Rin gleefully asked the three remaining contestants' ridiculous question after ridiculous question.

"What difference does it make if they prefer a pool or a hot tub?" Reagan scoffed as she sank further into her seat. Folded arms creased her cotton tee.

The Single in the City live show was the last place she wanted to be, yet thanks to Miller's insistence she support their friend, Reagan was slumped into the second seat from the aisle.

As if simply knowing Deacon was moving on wasn't torment enough, she was forced to watch the progression with her very own eyes.

Not that she could explain that problem to her brother.

Reagan's fingers met her throbbing temples. An auditorium full of delirious fans screaming at the athlete's every word enhanced her pulsing headache.

One could argue that she didn't have a right to be upset since she'd turned down his offer of a relationship a few evenings prior, but what other choice did she have?

Miller wouldn't want them to be together.

Stella didn't approve.

The universe had made it more than clear that they needed to keep their distance.

How could they overcome that level of opposition?

They couldn't.

Especially not in a world where happy endings were few and far between.

"These questions are ludicrous. Deacon has to be cringing inside knowing that people are trying to select his date based on such petty things," Reagan jeered.

Why was no one else appalled by Rin's queries?

As Deacon's best friend, wasn't Miller supposed to protect him from unworthy women?

"All relationships begin with the simple stuff," Miller replied. "You have to start somewhere."

"It's true." Kate's blue eyes twinkled with a fond memory as she leaned over Miller's armrest, draping her hand across his forearm. "Miller and I started with math."

"Math?" Reagan's eyebrow rose over her glassy stare.

Her wild brother had bonded with his girlfriend over something so boring as calculations?

Love was crazier than she thought.

With a matching gleam, Miller wrapped Kate's hand in his own, pulling her knuckles to his lips. "And I've never been more grateful for second grade homework."

"No, I'm the one that's thankful," Kate said, swooping her fingers over his floppy hair. "That was the night everything changed, and I saw how kind and caring you truly are."

"I'm just lucky you saw beyond my past," Miller replied, lips pressing against his girlfriend's cheek. "I love you."

Reagan shifted her slouch, angling toward Kai and away from her brother. "You two are sickening."

That wasn't the only thing making Reagan nauseous. The idea of Deacon with another woman made her stomach churn.

It was worse knowing that she'd put him in that position. Reagan thought his participation would be best for everyone, but it was turning out to be the opposite. She was miserable.

But she had no choice but to sit and suffer through it or she'd risk raising her brother's suspicion.

Reagan's gaze wandered back to the stage where Deacon was laughing with Rin. After several years in the spotlight, the athlete hid his stage fright well. But Reagan knew him too intimately to miss strains of his nervous chuckled splattered in the cackling mix.

It was hard to imagine that there was a time when she hadn't known all of his tics. In fact, she'd known Deacon for so long, she wasn't even sure where they began. She couldn't remember a time when she didn't know that he preferred his burgers with onion and cheese only or that he actually liked water without ice.

Falling across the armrest, Kai leaned over to Reagan while glancing to the doting couple in the adjacent seats. "You haven't even seen the worst of them, you know. They kiss *all* of the time."

"Apparently, that's your fault," Reagan said, flicking his arm in a playful jest. "You brought them together, so you deserve to suffer with the rest of us."

"You can't blame a kid." Kai pulled his hands to his shirt. "I didn't know what I was doing."

Reagan lifted her index finger. "False. You were always pushing Miller to get a girlfriend."

"So? Everybody needs somebody special." Kai's brown eyes glanced at Reagan. "Except you, I guess. You only need me and Miller."

"You're special enough for me." Reagan sighed, wrapping her arm around the back of Kai's chair.

"I am pretty cool," Kai said.

"So cool no one else can compare," Reagan replied. "Besides, I think I work better alone."

At least, she had at one point in time. Though, with each passing day, she couldn't help but wonder if it were still true.

"Is that why you're thinking about leaving us?" Kai's sad eyes flashed up at Reagan.

Reagan's forehead wrinkled. "Who said anything about leaving?"

"I overheard you and Kate talking the other night," Kai said, lip curling with sorrow. "You said you were moving on."

Reagan nodded with understanding as she squeezed the young boy's shoulders. "I meant that I'm making some changes in my personal life. Not leaving town."

While Reagan didn't want to disappoint Kai with her departure, the idea of relocating didn't sound terrible. Switching base stations would provide separation from Deacon and preserve her relationship with Miller before it was shattered to a point of no repair.

Before she broke him.

Reagan's gaze shifted back to her brother and Kate whose heads were huddled together, whispers floating between their smiles. Her heart leapt with a joyful patter at the sight of their affection.

Miller had earned this moment in his life, and Reagan couldn't be the one to ruin it.

Her head nodded toward Kate and Miller. "Maybe the torture is worth it since they're happy?"

"Yeah. Probably," Kai conceded.

"You do know we can hear you?" Miller cut in.

"You do know people can see you?" Reagan replied.

"People always watch me. May as well give them something good to talk about," Miller smirked. "Besides, isn't this whole show supposed to be about love?"

Reagan's jeans shifted against the thick leather padding. "Deacon doesn't *love* any of these women."

At least, she hoped not.

She wasn't ready for that yet.

Reagan didn't wish him a lifetime alone, but she needed time to process what Deacon dating someone else looked like. Her brain needed to figure out how to see him as a friend again and nothing more.

Even if her heart disagreed.

"I think he's too confused to love them," Miller said. "He still seems to be riding the fence. Like he's not quite sure which way to go between the contestants and his mystery woman."

"I suppose he's being cautious," Reagan said.

She, more than anyone, understood the sentiment. One couldn't be too careful when it came to such a strong emotion. Love was a fickle beast who would tear a person apart if they weren't careful. That's why she'd taken great care to avoid it over the years.

"More like a moron." Miller's head shook in disagreement. "When it comes to matter of the heart, you're on one side of the fence or the other. You can't ride the middle line. That just leaves you stuck."

Brow creasing, Reagan nipped at her nail as a flurry of upbeat music sprang from the speakers.

"Once again, the votes are in," Rin announced, waving a pink envelope through the air. "The winner of this week's one on one date is . . ."

Playing the part of a good host, Rin paused to let the excitement build before she pulled the card from its nest. She stamped her feet against the floor, encouraging the audience to join in.

A rumble shook the ground as audience members took the bait.

Reagan's heart picked up a beat as her mind echoed fervent prayers.

Not her. Not her. Not her.

Anyone but her.

"Saachi," Rin announced, confirming Reagan's fear.

Clapping and cheers erupted as Saachi beamed with delight from atop her stool. With shoulders back, and legs crossed at the ankle, she waved to the audience as would a queen from her carriage.

A loopy smile formed on Deacon's face as his hands joined the applause.

Was Miller wrong?

Had Deacon hopped down from the fence and onto Saachi's side?

Despite sitting in a chair bolted to the floor, Reagan's stomach twisted as if she were plummeting from the highest peak of a roller coaster barreling back to solid ground.

The wretched feeling of watching Deacon be happy with another woman was unlike anything she'd ever experienced. Heat flushed her cheeks, yet she felt a chill at her core. All consuming agony clutched her chest and torturous palpitations beat against her brain.

"Are you okay?" Miller's face wrinkled as he turned to his sister. "You look like you're going to be sick."

Without a word, Reagan scrambled up from her seat, climbed over Kai, and made haste for the door.

She wasn't ill.

No.

Illness could be cured.

It was much worse than that.

There was no remedy for her ailment.

Reagan was in love.

And it was as miserable as she imagined.

Chapter Twenty-two

FEET pounding against the concrete floor, Reagan raced backstage. A husky man in a black polo was posted by the side door, but that didn't deter the flight attendant from her course. Her chest throbbed with painful breaths, yet Reagan didn't slow her pace.

She had to catch Deacon before he left on his date with Saachi.

Had to stop him from making a huge mistake.

Reagan sprinted past the security guard, who shouted a few words, but ending up waving off her breach. Perhaps her and Deacon's bad luck streak was ending?

Spotting Deacon darting into the men's dressing room, Reagan followed his move and ducked inside the prep area. Bright bulbs circled the mirrors, causing the flight attendant's eyes to taper upon entry.

"Reagan?" Deacon's lashes flashed a double beat as if he might be imagining her presence. His lips opened and closed several times before he muttered, "What are you doing back here?"

"We . . ." she heaved, falling to the loveseat as she attempted to catch her breath, "have to talk."

Deacon took a few steps closer, concern lacing his voice. "Are you okay?"

"No," Reagan's head shook against the pewter fabric lining the cushions. "No, I'm not."

Her knees felt weak.

Her chest was heavy.

Her heart wretched.

All because she was about to lose a man she loved.

Loved.

How was the even possible? She'd fought so hard against it, yet Deacon somehow managed to pierce her steel exterior.

Sensing her distress, the athlete took a knee and bent to her level, his palm rounding the side of her thigh. "What's wrong?"

"This." Reagan's arms opened to the walls plastered with posters from past performances. "All of this."

Deacon's thumb brushed over the hole in her jeans. "What are you talking about?"

"The show. The women." Reagan's hands cupped his cheeks as she bent her upper body toward his. "It's just wrong. I can't take it anymore. You can't go on this date tonight."

Deacon's cutting gaze burrowed into her own. "Why not?"

"Because . . ." she gulped.

I love you.

Reagan's mind yelled the words her lips couldn't say. It was too much. Verbalizing her feelings would make her too vulnerable. It would give Deacon the control. The power to hurt her. And she couldn't risk that.

"I don't like it." Reagan said, her eyes falling to the floor. "I hate seeing these women fawn all over you."

Deacon's head shook with disappointment as he pushed her hands away. Reagan knew it wasn't what he wanted to hear, but she couldn't give him more. It was bad enough that she loved him. Her heart couldn't take the pain of him knowing.

Deacon lifted to his feet as his hands grazed his head. "I'm not sure why you're putting on the jealous act when we both know this is what you wanted."

He was right. She had encouraged his participation in the show, but now, she realized that she'd been wrong. Reagan didn't want Deacon to move on. He was supposed to be with her.

Only her.

"It's not an act," she argued. "I don't like you spending time with her. Or any of them for that matter."

Unlatching the button atop his suit coat, Deacon tossed the garment to the back of the chair. "You're always flipping between hot and cold when it comes to us, and right now just happens to be a hot moment because you know I'm about to go on a date with Saachi. But you'll be back to frigid tomorrow morning. Just like always."

"No, I won't. I know what I want now." Reagan sprung to a standing position. Wrapping her arms around his waist, her head dropped to Deacon's chest. The steady thump of his heart was a metronome guiding her racing pulse to slow.

"That's good for you." Deacon's palm smoothed her hair as he pressed a kiss to the top of her head before resting his cheek against her soft strands. "But I can't say the same."

"Why not?" Reagan's torso pulled back as her chin lifted to Deacon's woeful expression.

"A lot has changed in the last few weeks. My world is spinning out of control, and I'm really confused about what is up and what is down."

"Meaning?"

She was still Reagan.

He was still Deacon.

And they belonged together.

What was there to be confused about?

"Exactly what I said." Deacon held her gaze without as much as a single blink of hesitation. "This experience has taught me a lot about myself and what I want, and I'm trying to find steady footing in my new path."

"Which leads where?"

"I don't know, but I know it holds more than a secret," Deacon said.

Reagan's throat tightened at his statement. He wanted more than her. Someone who could be his date to events. A woman he could share a glass of wine with at a restaurant. Someone like . . .

"Saachi," Reagan breathed.

Deacon's shoulders lifted. "I don't know. Maybe."

"So even if I asked you to quit . . ."

Shifting his gaze to the floor, Deacon's shoes scraped the black, tile floor. "I can't quit the show, Rea."

The flight attendant's lashes bit back the sting of disappointment that welled on her lower lids. "Can't or won't?"

"It's not that simple. There are other people to consider."

"Like?"

"Stella. She would throttle me if I quit. And the underprivileged children. This is a huge fundraiser for them. I can't bail on that. Plus, Saachi has a lot riding on the show, too. I don't want to let her down."

It was one thing to be scared of Stella. Everyone was.

Reagan could even justify Deacon wanting to help at risk children.

But Saachi?

Why was she suddenly part of the equation?

When had her stock become worth more than Reagan's?

A single tear streamed down her flushed cheek. "So you'll let me down instead?"

Deacon tugged at the knot wrapping his neck. "I'm not letting you down. I'm just not doing exactly what you want, and you're not used to that. I always cave for you, Rea." Freeing the silk from his collar, Deacon's head shook. "But not this time. This time we do things my way."

"So what? I just have to wait around while you date other people?"

Deacon's feet paused at the brim of the doorway. His head turned back to the small space as a grievous glaze frosted his brown eyes. "I've been waiting on you for months, so I'm pretty sure you can handle a few weeks."

With that, the athlete sauntered away, leaving the sting of his words to bite at Reagan's crumbling heart.

Was her realization too late?

Had Deacon's heart passed to another?

And what was she going to do if it had?

Chapter Twenty-three

THE last streaks of reddish-pink hovered on the horizon as Deacon and Saachi exited the historic, downtown auditorium.

It came as no surprise that the audience had once again selected Saachi for the one on one date. Deacon even found himself sighing a breath of relief at Rin's announcement. Saachi possessed a calming presence which Deacon was in great need of considering how poorly things were going with Reagan.

If they were even going at all after their encounter in the dressing room.

Deacon hadn't meant to discard her sudden desire to be together. But at the same time, he couldn't accept Reagan's supposed change of heart without knowing if she was still going to feel the same way tomorrow.

Of course, she wanted him in the midst of a jealous rage, but what about when it was just a regular Saturday? Would she want him then?

And did he really want her knowing that they'd only ever be a secret? What kind of life was lived behind closed doors?

Once upon a time, Deacon thought he could accept such a fate, but now that he knew he had another option, he wasn't so sure.

"You okay?" Saachi asked, looping an arm around Deacon's bicep.

The athlete attempted to focus his attention to the woman beside him, instead of the one who haunted his mind.

Dark denim and a white v-neck replaced his date's flowy dress. While the yellow number had flattered her skin color and fine figure, Deacon preferred laid-back living. That's why he'd told the women to pack a casual outfit in case they won the solo outing. And the athlete wasn't surprised to find Saachi looked just as good dressed down.

Maybe even better.

"Just tired," Deacon said, trying to live in the moment. "That's all."

He didn't want to ruin Saachi's night just because he and Reagan had an argument. It wasn't fair to punish her for their mistakes. Especially when she might be the one waiting at the end of his new path.

"We can skip the date tonight if you need," Saachi said, searching Deacon's face as if it hid the answers to his frame of mind. "I'll understand."

"I appreciate the offer, but it's not necessary. I'll rally."

Stepping ahead of his date, Deacon popped the handle on the pewter, four door pickup parked near the secret side exit. Thick, thirty-five inch mud tires lifted the cab higher than the standard fare, so Deacon was grateful for his height.

"A truck?" Saachi's curious eyes glanced from the pickup to the athlete as her Keds stepped onto the chrome running board. Pulling up on the arm rest, she hopped into the leather coated passenger seat. "It's quite nice, but I didn't take you for the type."

"I'm not," Deacon chuckled, holding the door open. "It belongs to Rook. He's from some middle of nowhere, farm town a few hours away, and he can't shake his redneck roots. But it plays to our favor tonight."

A curious glow lit Saachi's eyes. "Care to share why?"

"Nope. It's a surprise."

With that Deacon closed the cab and bound behind the steering wheel. Exhaust rumbling, six cylinders roared through the bright downtown streets until the truck veered off to darker roads, headed for the countryside.

He'd first scouted their destination for a date with Reagan, but seeing as they'd never progressed to public outings, the rural haven remained untouched.

Deacon debated saving it for the future, but Reagan's wishy washy behavior always made it impossible to know if tomorrow even existed for them.

Tonight she wanted him to quit the dating show.

To make a sacrifice for her.

For them.

Yet any time he suggested they become more than friends, she scoffed at the idea like he was crazy.

Which maybe she was right? Maybe he was insane.

Only a mad man would keep loving a woman who would never love him in return when there was a perfectly wonderful woman perched in the seat right next to him. A beautiful one, at that.

One who seemed interested in spending time with him. One who cared what he thought. What he felt.

Deacon peeked at Saachi as her fingers combed through her long, dark locks. Catching his brief stare, her lashes batted over her amber eye in a playful wink.

What did he feel?

Deacon's fingers brushed his freshly shaved jaw. Over the last year, he'd worked hard to find inner peace and clarity in the midst of the discord created by his and Reagan's lies.

He'd managed successfully for a while. But every day since the dating show began, a sliver of Deacon's former lucidity had slipped way, and he was left with the harsh clamor of mixed emotions.

He wasn't supposed to like Saachi.

Wasn't supposed to feel anything for her.

Yet, Deacon couldn't stop the pounding of his heart every time she smiled in his direction.

Did that make him a cheater? Was it even considered cheating when you wanted to be with someone who didn't want you back?

And why was he holding on to a relationship where he even had to debate such a situation?

"If there weren't cameras in the truck and a film crew stalking us in a van, I think I might be a bit concerned right now." Saachi's voice broke Deacon's solemn trance as her jeans shifted in the seat. Her seatbelt tugged at her chest as she peered out the window at the freshly planted fields where green buds sprouted from the soil. "You seem upset, and I feel like I've seen this scene in a horror movie."

"No fear necessary," Deacon said, pointing ahead. "We're almost there."

Saachi's head turned to take in the panoramic view of fields and aged trees. "Where is *there?*"

"You'll see," Deacon said with a faint smile.

It was amusing, he decided, surprising someone with an outing. Even if it wasn't the person he originally anticipated.

A green blinker arrow clicked as the truck turned onto a small town main street. Brick buildings filled with local shops rolled by before the tires curled to a gravel drive.

Deacon piped up again as they approached the vintage, blue Starlight sign. His hands tapped a beat against the leather steering wheel. "I'm a little tired of the limelight, so I thought we'd hide out in the dark tonight and let other people be the stars."

Saachi squealed with delight as her palm shook Deacon's bicep. "I've never been to the drive-in before, but I've always wanted to go."

Deacon's heart leapt at Saachi's excitement. He'd forgotten how it felt to go on a real date. To be with a woman and not have to worry about discovery. To shower someone with the time and attention they wanted.

A grin brightened Deacon's face as he slipped a twenty to the teen collecting money at the gate. "Well, according to Rook, there's no better way to watch a movie than from the bed of a truck."

"I imagine that's true if you have good company," Saachi said, scrunching her nose as they rolled down the gravel drive. "Otherwise, it could be rather awkward."

Deacon's arm wound behind the passenger seat as he backed into a spot. "Well then, I guess I'm lucky the audience picked you."

His palm kept hold of the cool leather as his gaze shifted to the woman sitting beside him. A few weeks ago, he'd thought she and the show would help him resolve his complicated love story. And in a sense, they had.

However, Deacon hadn't expected that they might also bring a beginning to a new story.

Saachi's long lashes lifted to reveal solemn amber stones. "You weren't hoping for someone else were you? I mean, I hoped you wouldn't be disappointed that you were stuck with me again."

"Of course, not." Deacon slid the gear into park before his elbow leaned to the middle arm rest. His body slanted toward Saachi and the tips of his lips lifted further in an attempt to reassure her wandering thoughts. "I enjoy spending time with you. You're easy."

Lips parting in false offense, Saachi slapped Deacon's arm with playful passivity. "Easy? How would you know? You haven't even kissed me yet! Much less, tried more."

"I meant simple," Deacon chuckled, holding his hands up in a sign of peace like he'd learned in fifth grade karate. "And not in an uneducated way," he added, correcting himself before she could fake offense again. "As in you're *easy* to be with. You make me feel . . . relaxed."

Saachi's fingers fluttered over Deacon's rigid knuckles. "If I make you feel relaxed, then I'm obviously doing something wrong."

Hand sweeping to the latch, Saachi unfastened her seat belt with a click. The shining metal latch glinted sparkling beams captured from the overhead projector, demanding Deacon's attention. His eyes followed the gleam as it drug over Saachi's subtle curves with turtle like slowness.

Deacon's palm met the back of his sweaty neck. "Perhaps that was the wrong phrasing as well."

The athlete reminded himself it wasn't polite to stare, but Saachi's sluggish pace all but demanded he study the shadow resting at the crook of her chest. Wonder about the plushness of the round peaks hovering on either side. Her voluptuous form varied greatly from Reagan's slim cut.

Not better.

Not worse.

Just different.

But then again, everything about Saachi was different.

Blocking the athlete's view and calling his drifting attention upward, Saachi draped her tanned arms over the same center console, a soft smile forming on her plump lips. "Perhaps."

"Perhaps what?" Deacon's lashes blinked as he tried to recall their conversation.

Saachi's brows lifted as a bemused grin lit her face. "Your phrasing could have been better."

"I've never been good at public speaking," Deacon admitted, nodding to the lens mounted on the dash.

"Don't think about the cameras." Saachi said, leaning in further. "Live in the moment with me."

The athlete's veins pulsed with a sudden yearning as her upper body inched toward his. The once large cab was growing smaller by the second. But not because the athlete was repulsed. In fact, it was quite the opposite. He'd thought Saachi was gorgeous from the moment he laid eyes on her, but it hadn't mattered then. She'd been a stranger.

But now, she was familiar. Kind. Understanding.

"I can try to pretend like we're insulated," Deacon replied, wincing with the realization that he'd minced his words again. "I mean, isolated."

"You aren't having the best of luck with speaking tonight," Saachi said, curving forward inch by inch. "So perhaps we should occupy your beautiful lips before you let anything else slip."

Guiding his chin with the gentle pull of her finger, Saachi's exquisite mouth drifted toward Deacon's. Her warm breath hovered over his lips, waiting for him to bridge the small gap.

The athlete thought about pulling back. Hopping out of the truck to go get a cold drink, or ice cream, or something equally cooling to squash the heat rising in the air between them. But Saachi's magnetism was pulling with a force he couldn't avoid.

Besides, he was supposed to be moving on. Exploring his options. When she'd been thinking rationally, Reagan had insisted on it.

Reagan.

What was he going to do about Reagan?

Deacon's lids slammed shut.

There wasn't anything he could do.

His heart still loved her, but his head... well, his head remembered that she wanted this for him. She'd pushed him into it. Into Saachi's hands.

Her very smooth hands which were now skimming the back of his neck. Enticing him to release his inhibition and close the small divide.

Inhibitions that were no longer necessary, the athlete reminded himself, seeing as he was moving on. Progressing to a relationship where he would be wanted for more than a moment.

With a hard swallow rippling down his throat, Deacon's lips drifted toward Saachi's, capturing her mouth in a warm embrace.

Her lips were different than he was used to, thicker where Reagan's were thin. Yet, they were soft and welcoming. Nice even. Brushing with an enthusiasm Deacon had missed. An excitement he could get used to. Yet, lacking the spark he'd grown accustomed to feeling.

Perhaps that came with time?

Or maybe the cool mint on her breath was deceiving him into believing there wasn't a heat building between them?

Roping Saachi's strands through his fingers, Deacon pulled her closer, hoping to be replenished with her passion.

Wanting.

And receiving.

Because Saachi wasn't leaving.

The athlete's tongue delved deeper, matching Saachi's enthusiasm in order to bolster his own. Her fingers caressed his chest and moved up to his shoulders with a featherlike brush that should have been maddening. If she were someone else.

Deacon pulled back, regretting his experiment. An aching of wrongfulness crept through his bones.

"That was . . ." Saachi's lids blinked with rapid amazement as her chest endeavored to regain steady breathing. "Different than I expected."

"Agreed," Deacon said.

"We just have so much in common, I guess I thought . . ."

"There should have been fireworks. Finale, end of the show stuff."

"I suppose that would have been too unreal, though."

"What do you mean?" Deacon's brow furrowed as his gaze met Saachi's.

"Oh, come on. You're beyond successful, handsome, and kind,"

Saachi waved a hand over Deacon's bent form. "If you kissed like the devil it would have been too good to be true."

"Why?"

Saachi's fingers looped her dark strands behind her ear. "Life is never that easy."

"I wish it were," Deacon said.

"I don't," Saachi said. "That would take all the fun out of it."

"It would?"

"Most certainly," Saachi said, cupping Deacon's cheek. "For instance, I plan to have quite a bit of fun practicing kissing you until we get it just right."

Her mouth hovered over his once more.

"So you're not giving up on this?" Deacon asked.

"You're not the kind of guy a girl gives up on," Saachi replied, nipping at his lips once more.

If only that were true.

Noticing his lack of reciprocation, Saachi pulled away. "Unless I'm fighting for something that isn't available."

"I don't know," Deacon replied, his head shaking. "I honestly don't know."

"Because of the woman that you mentioned at our first dinner . . ."

Deacon's head gave a slight nod.

"Can I ask who?" Saachi sighed, her dark eyes flashing in his direction. "A girlfriend? Ex-wife? The high school sweetheart you still pine for?"

"An ex, I suppose. The labels were never very clear," Deacon said, folding his arms over his lightweight tee. "But I don't know why I care. It's a cliché tale of unrequited love."

"The worst kind," Saachi said.

"Especially when you have mutual friends." Deacon's head wavered. "Ones who don't even know we were together."

"You didn't want them to find out?" Saachi's chin lifted in understanding.

Deacon's hands tapped the wood with a nervous drum. "Like I said, it's complicated."

"A secret relationship couldn't be anything else," Saachi said.

Deacon's head nodded in agreement. The stakes had been stacked against them from the start. How had he ever been so naive to think that he and Reagan could evolve into something more while they were still in hiding?

"Do you love her?" she asked.

Deacon flashed to Reagan curled on Miller's couch in a sweatshirt and yoga pants the first night he met her. Saw her smiling and waving a peanut butter cookie as her animated hands accentuated her story-telling. He remembered how her eyes sparkled with laughter and simple happiness.

Looking back, the athlete could see his descent into enthrallment began that very moment. And now. Now it was so much more.

"Unfortunately." Deacon's lashes fluttered with his admission. "But it doesn't matter because—"

"Consequences," Saachi said, as if she had the ability to read his mind. "But if you really want to be with her, surely there has to be some way around it? Something that could appease the naysayers."

Deacon sighed. He'd spent hours upon hours contemplating the same scenario. But despite his best efforts, no reasonable solution had been uncovered.

"Short of marriage, no, I don't think so."

Saachi's lips pursed, parted, closed, and then opened again. "But if you got married, you think that the offended party or parties would accept your relationship?"

"I think he'd still be a bit peeved, but it would alleviate his concern of us breaking up." Deacon's palm brushed his scalp. "She and I . . . we can't get married, though. We've never even been on a date."

Saachi's fingers combed through her thick locks. "People date to get to know each other, and it sounds to me like you already know this woman well."

"I suppose you have a point," Deacon said. "But proposing still seems like jumping off the high dive before taking a practice round on a lower rung."

"Maybe. But if you're not willing to do something crazy to keep her, then she's not the one," Saachi said.

She was right.

True love called for drastic measures.

And luckily, there was still time for a hail Mary play. But Deacon couldn't win the game alone. He had to see if Reagan wanted to be on his team.

Forever.

Chapter Twenty-four

REAGAN couldn't peel her eyes away from the glowing screen as she watched Deacon's kiss with Saachi unfold on the screen once more. Even at the third play through, her chest was heavy with grief. However, in contrast to the first viewing of their passionate embrace, her tears had been shocked into submission.

Deacon's earlier rejection was no longer a question of why. Now, it was clear. He'd selected Saachi.

The athlete had taken her in his strong arms and claimed her as the one he wanted in front of the entire viewing audience.

In front of her.

Even worse, their entanglement must have moved to the next heat level because the video stream came to an abrupt halt at their kiss. No doubt because the Public Education Foundation didn't want to be associated with illicit behavior. Nor did they want to ruin the surprise of who would win in the end. Even if the answer was abundantly clear.

Saachi.

Saachi would take Deacon's heart and everything he had to offer. Everything that had once been hers.

Reagan slammed the lid on her laptop shut just as a knock sounded on the door of Miller's apartment.

She didn't need to answer it to know who was standing behind the wood plank. Miller and Kate were at her place, Kai was at home, and Miller's housekeeper kept daytime hours. There was only one other person who had clearance to come up without pre-approval.

Deacon.

Had he come to gloat to Miller about his conquest?

Flaunt it in her face that he had been able to move on so easily?

Reagan twisted the deadbolt, but left the chain lock in place as she cracked the door. Without looking at Deacon she voiced, "Miller is at Kate's."

"I didn't come for him." A twinge of desperation squeaked through his tone.

"Then, I don't know why you're here," Reagan said. "You made your point earlier, so there's nothing much left to say."

"That's not entirely true," Deacon said, cinching his sneaker into the door's opening, so she couldn't slam it shut. "Please, let me come in. We need to talk."

Peeking through the small gap, Reagan's eyes flitted to Deacon's hollow expression. His skin paled with guilt and his eyes held a glassy sadness.

Had he really come to see her?

What did that mean?

Out of instinct, Reagan's hand started to reach out to comfort the athlete, but not yet sure if he was hers to comfort, she gripped the metal knob instead. Swinging the door open, Reagan allowed Deacon to pass.

Hurrying through the entryway, he made a quick pivot back toward Reagan. "I might have a solution to our problem."

Hope soaring to her heart, Reagan's pulse picked up a beat. "Really?"

"Yes." Deacon hovered over her form, his voice softening.

"But what about Saachi?" she stammered, hand wrapping the back of her neck. "You had your date. I saw you kiss."

"We did, but it was . . . I don't know . . . *weird.*"

"First kisses often are," Reagan said.

"It was more than that. She wasn't you." Deacon's forehead sank meet Reagan's. "I told Saachi my heart was with someone else."

"Why would you do that?" Reagan whispered, tension rising in her throat.

Had he really given up his perfect match for her?

"It's the truth," Deacon replied, wrapping her hands with his own. His fierce gaze pierced her own. "I came here to show you that I'm willing to do whatever it takes to be with you, and that's what I'm going to do."

Reagan's lashes fluttered. "But you hate lying to Miller."

"I hate not having you more."

Deacon's lips brushed against the corner of her lips with soft reverence.

Reagan's hands jittered with nervous excitement. "I don't understand, you said you wanted more than a secret."

"I do," Deacon said.

"But how?" Reagan's head shook with confusion. "Even if Miller did approve, he'd be so paranoid about us breaking up that he would hound us until we wanted to break up."

"What if there was no question of our longevity?" Deacon asked.

How could that be? Reagan's mind raced through ideas, but none fit the bill.

"There's always the possibility of breaking up," Reagan replied.

Deacon dipped to kiss her lips once more, his heated breath warming her lips as he pulled away. "Not if you marry me."

Eyes bugged, Reagan turned toward the athlete, her voice lifting. "Marriage?"

Holy matrimony.

The commitment she'd sworn she'd never make.

"It makes perfect sense," Deacon said, a grin growing on his lips. "Miller can't argue that level of commitment. It would show him we're not just fooling around."

"But that's exactly what we've been doing," Reagan replied, brow wrinkling.

"Only because we didn't know how to be more and keep the peace with Miller."

Reagan's heart sank to her feet.

Marriage might keep the peace with Miller. But what about harmony for them? For their lives?

Newlywed bliss would fade after a few months, and then they'd be left with conflict and heartbreak.

Forever.

As if he could read her nervousness, Deacon tugged Reagan's body closer. "If you really think about it, marriage is the logical solution."

"Marriage is never logical," Reagan said, pulling back. "Especially not when you skip all of the steps to getting there. I mean, we've never even been on a real date."

"People date to get to know each other. We've far surpassed that." Deacon layered two soft kisses on her knuckles. "Besides, if we can get through this past few months of not really dating, I know we can make a legitimate relationship work."

"How can you know that?" Reagan lifted to her feet and paced for the kitchen counter, gripping the cool granite as she attempted to calm her reeling mind.

How could anyone jump into a commitment where the success rate was less than fifty percent?

If a surgery boasted those odds, people would use extreme caution with their decision making. But with marriage, it seemed no one gave the poor standings a second thought.

"How can you be so sure?" she asked again.

The athlete's long legs stripped the distance between them, placing a reassuring hand at her back. "I know what we have isn't usual."

Reagan's face turned to Deacon, eyes filled with fear. "And what if you change your mind in a few years? What happens when you decide you don't want this anymore? That it's not special?"

"That won't happen." Deacon's thumb brushed against her spine. "These aren't the kind of feelings that fade."

"They might. I've seen it play out just like that."

Deacon's hand wiped over his face. "I'm not those guys. You know I'm different."

"I doubt my mother thought my father would wander," Reagan said, turning to the athlete, fear lacing her eyes. "But he did."

Agitation grew in Deacon's voice. "So I have to pay for his sins?"

"No," Reagan said, placing her palm over Deacon's heart. "You're free to live your life and be happy."

With someone else.

The words went unspoken, but the truth hung in the air like thick smog.

It would hurt to watch his future relationship blossom. But deep down, Reagan knew that pain was miniscule in comparison to what Deacon could do to her heart if they were foolish enough to get married.

And how many heartbreaks could a girl suffer before one finally did her in?

Eyes turning to the floor, Reagan moved for the foyer where three, cardboard boxes sat. Lifting shirts from the nearby chair, she stuffed the stack inside a container.

Tears clung to the rim of her lids, but her lashes beat them back.

In a few weeks, her transfer to Chicago would be complete, and two hundred miles would serve as the sedative to soothe her wounded soul.

"But I won't be happy without you," Deacon called, eyeing the collection at the doorway.

"And I won't be happy in a marriage." Reagan turned back to Deacon. "I can't chance losing everything the way my mother did."

She was hurting enough as it was, and their relationship wasn't even solidified. Reagan couldn't imagine what kind of pain one would suffer after losing someone they'd promised forever to.

"You're already losing everything," Deacon said, lifting her chin. "How do you not see that?"

Reagan's lids raised up to meet the athlete's grave stare. "I have to do what I think is best. I'm allowed to lookout for myself."

"You're not looking out. You're running scared, and we both know it," Deacon said, watery eyes darting down the dimly lit corridor.

"You ran first," Reagan said, a single tear streaking her cheek. "That night in Atlanta. You couldn't get away from me fast enough."

"Because I felt like I was betraying my best friend," Deacon argued. "I didn't know how I could have both of you."

"And what about the dating show? You didn't seem to mind that Stella signed you up."

"I thought it would make you jealous, but I guess I was wrong," Deacon clipped. "You're hell bent on keeping everyone at an arm's length."

"Can you blame me? A few weeks ago, you said you'd wait forever for me, yet you were more than happy to pick up with Saachi when things got tough."

"You seriously think I'm the problem?" Deacon's hands brushed over his head as his glare grew rigid. "You've made this an impossible obstacle course."

"To protect myself from moments like this and indecisive men like you," Reagan replied, her hand whipping between them.

"A moment *you* caused by telling me I should move on time and time again. If you had been willing to go all in, we wouldn't be here." Deacon's hands pushed off the door frame, pausing after a few steps. "Your dad may have messed up your childhood with his choices, but you're ruining the rest with your own."

Reagan's heart skipped a beat as the reality of his statement hit her ears.

Her father's departure had defined her youth, so she'd allowed his actions to determine her own. Used the hurt to guard her heart.

But Deacon was right. Reagan had created the storm she was living in. Somehow, in trying to protect herself from men like her father, she had become him.

And to what gain?

She had a job where personal connections lasted no more than a few hours.

Her closed off personality kept potential friends at bay.

Romantic interests as well.

Everyone.

Even the best man she'd ever known.

The man who just offered her forever despite her flaws.

"Deacon—" Reagan's feet took two steps forward, her lashes batting back tears.

She hadn't meant to hurt him. She'd wanted to save him from the terrible pain love often brought with it.

Yet, his bloodshot eyes indicated she'd failed at doing so.

"Don't."

Deacon held out a flat palm as he hit the elevator's call button and Reagan jerked to a halt.

He'd pushed her away before, but this time was different. There was no anxious jitter in his hands, or flustered breath heaving in his chest. The towering man before her was stoic. Sure. As if there were no doubt in his mind he was making the right choice.

"I've never been one to accept a loss," Deacon said, "but I'm done with this game. You win."

"How do I win?" Reagan's throat tightened at his dismissal.

Deacon shoved his hands in his pockets. "I'm giving you what you wanted. A life alone."

Without so much as a backward glance, Deacon disappeared from the hallway.

Reagan's hands covered her watering face as she sank to the floor.

If this was winning, why was she miserable?

Chapter Twenty-five

HIKING across the city sidewalks, Deacon's chin lifted to the stars shining bright against the cloak of midnight. Over the course of his hour long meandering, the spring sky had maintained its unblemished condition without a cloudy haze in sight.

But how could that be?

Nothing was clear in Deacon's life anymore. Everything that once made sense was now enveloped in a murky fog. And his heart . . .

Deacon's head wavered.

Did he even have a heart anymore? He was sure he'd felt it fly from his chest the moment Reagan rejected his proposal.

Though he shouldn't have been surprised. Deacon knew better than to believe Reagan would ever settle down. He'd held out hope she would go against Miller's wishes, not wanting to accept the reality that they might not end up together.

But now, there was no more denying it.

They were through, and after running one last Hail Mary play, he only had one option left.

He had to move on.

Shoving through the double doors of his complex's lobby, Deacon passed by the elevator and made for the stairway. Five flights of steps taken two at a time would set his calves on fire but at least he'd know he still had the ability to feel something other than the overwhelming numbness that had spread throughout his body.

Metal clanked as Deacon pulled keys from his pockets. Feeling the emotional fatigue of a long day, he wanted nothing more than to pour a stiff drink, collapse on his soft mattress, and try to forget the day Reagan Cassidy stumbled into his life.

"Have you lost your damn mind?"

Deacon cringed when he heard Stella's cutting voice echo through the cracked door of his apartment.

Hadn't he suffered enough for one night?

"Ironic coming from the person breaking and entering," Deacon snipped, kicking off his sneakers in the dim foyer.

The athlete wanted to be surprised that she'd weaseled her way into his home, but Deacon had been with the Panther's long enough to know better.

Arms crossed and face scowling, Stella sat propped in the recliner that faced the door. She donned a vee neck t-shirt and faded jeans, but Deacon knew her casual attire wouldn't translate to her attitude.

"I borrowed Miller's spare," Stella said, dangling the silver keychain as her narrowed gaze zoomed in on Deacon's form. "And you're lucky I'm only breaking into your apartment. I should snap your legs for that little stunt you pulled this evening."

The public relation shark's eyebrows lifted and dared him to contradict.

Bleached by the fluorescent lamps hovering on either side of the couch, her generally bronzed skin looked vampire pale. Deacon knew from experience she didn't need the extra illusion to be scary. Still, he didn't feel the need to tiptoe around Stella. He'd done more than enough of that lately, and Deacon was tired of being walked over by people who thought they knew best.

"I didn't pull any stunts," Deacon protested.

"So you didn't propose to Reagan Cassidy?" Stella's eyes widened with question as she slid to the edge of her seat. "Because there's a group text blowing up on my phone that implies otherwise."

"Oh, that." Deacon sighed as he fell into the plush couch, pulling a pillow to his chest. "It was more of a suggestion of marriage than a question."

Stella's lips pursed with displeasure. "Either way, I told you to stay away from her."

Deacon's gaze fell to the green material as he toyed with the crisply sewn edges. "I'm aware."

"Yet you *proposed?*" Stella snipped. "What were you thinking?"

A hard swallow raced down Deacon's throat.

He'd once considered himself a wise man, but when it came to Reagan, he'd never been able to see reason. He'd played the worst card in a hand he should have folded. In a game he should have walked away from.

"I thought it would fix the Miller issue."

Stella shot up from her seated position as her voiced boomed across the apartment. "Do you know what fixes the Miller issue? Staying the hell away from his sister."

"She said no, so it doesn't even matter," Deacon murmured, diverting his gaze away from the intruder, "She's too damn afraid of commitment."

Pausing in front of the darkened fireplace, Stella's hand met her hip. "Then, it's time to let her go."

"As if I ever had her." Deacon's head shook. "And here I thought the Single Series would make her see what she stood to lose. Such a stupid idea."

Stella's arms crossed as she sank to the armrest next to Deacon, a flash of empathy lighting her solemn eyes. "You know as well as I do that matters of the heart can't be manipulated."

As much as he hated her answer, Stella was right. No one could convince Reagan that love didn't have to leave hurt and pain in its wake. Nor could the jealousy that stemmed from his participation in the dating show lead her to realize that what they had was worth fighting for.

Sadness and regret turned in Deacon's stomach.

How could he have read the situation so wrong?

Chapter Twenty-six

"**A**RE you ready to go?"

Reagan's gaze turned for the doorway as Kate's head popped through the white frame of her bedroom door. A high pony revealed the curve of her neckline, left bare by a drooping, off-the-shoulder sweater.

"I'm staying here tonight." Redirecting her attention to a half packed cardboard box, the flight attendant continued to layer articles of clothing.

Packing for her pending move to Chicago wasn't an exciting Saturday night, but Reagan didn't care. The last place she wanted to be was in the same location as Deacon.

He hadn't given up on her for months.

But now, when she realized she was wrong about parting ways, Deacon thought she was right.

"I know you're having a tough time right now, but you can't skip a game," Kate argued, her arms folding as her shoulder met the wood border lining the door. "Nor do I think skipping town is the answer."

Reagan slid a picture frame between two stacks of shirts. "I'm an adult. I can do whatever I want."

Less than twenty-four hours ago she'd declined a marriage proposal. Surely, she could reject an invitation to a sporting event.

"Miller will be suspicious as to why you're absent."

Waving off Kate's concern, Reagan reached for the roll of packing tape. "After last night, I suspect Deacon will be such a disaster that Miller will hardly have time to notice my presence or lack thereof."

Kate's feet carried her a few steps into the room. "You only miss games when you're out of town. He'll know something is up if you aren't there."

"Something is *up*," Reagan said.

Or was it down?

She didn't even know any more. Her emotions were high. They were low. They were left. They were right.

Well, maybe not that.

Unfortunately, she hadn't done much right, lately.

She'd handled everything all wrong.

And everyone was suffering because of it.

Chapter Twenty-seven

"**W**HAT the hell, man?" Miller rubbed a white towel over his damp hair during their half time break. "We need five guys with their heads in the game in order to win."

Deacon took a swig of water as the pair navigated through the threshold of the locker room. "We can still make the playoffs. One loss isn't that big of a deal."

The Panther's had never charted a perfect season, so the veteran athlete didn't understand why it mattered now.

"I wouldn't think a thing of it if we were playing our best. But you . . ." Miller's head shook as he tossed his towel to the bottom of his locker. "I don't know where you've been tonight, but it isn't in this stadium."

"I've got a lot going on," Deacon argued, wiping his sweat stained brow with his jersey.

"We all have lives outside of basketball," Miller snipped. "But we still show up for games."

"I seem to remember you throwing brick after brick when things were rocky with Kate after the telethon. And I didn't give you a hard time about it."

"That was one game in pre-season," Miller argued, flopping in his seat. "You've been acting weird for weeks. I thought it was a passing phase, but I'm seriously starting to worry about you."

Deacon shuffled through his duffle bag in an attempt to ignore Miller's concern as he waited for their coach to come admonish him with the same scathing words.

"I'm fine," he lied.

Though, Deacon wasn't sure why he was still being untruthful to his best friend. There was nothing to lie about now.

"You are far from fine," Miller scoffed, kicking his feet up to Deacon's chair.

It was true, but who was Miller to point it out? How many times had he been off his game because life simply wouldn't let him be?

Deacon turned toward his teammate. "You've got no room to judge."

"I never said I did." Miller lifted his hands to the air. "But this isn't about me. So do you want to tell me what's really going on, or are you just going to make me guess?"

Deacon's arms folded across his chest as he plopped in an empty chair. He'd avoided telling his friend the truth for months, so what was the point in caving now? It would only make more of a mess.

"I can't help you if you don't tell me." Miller's feet hit the floor as his elbows met his knees.

"You can't help me if I do," Deacon replied, waving off Miller's request.

"If your best friend can't help, who can?"

"No one, man. That's the point." Deacon tossed a white towel over his head and sopped up sweat from his barely there hair. "I know you're into saving people now, but just leave me be."

An age old saying proclaimed misery liked company. But in this particular case, Deacon wanted nothing more than to be left alone with his agony. And if he had desired a companion, Miller wouldn't have ranked on the list of possible candidates. He reminded Deacon too much of Reagan.

Sure, the sibling's hair held different shades, and Miller's features favored their father while Reagan's favored their mother, but it went deeper than that. Their carefree nature and flippant disregard for boundaries was identical. And their smile. That cocky, half-grin that the Cassidy crew used as a weapon when they wanted to charm their way into or out of trouble.

That smile was Deacon's kryptonite. The reason he had gone down a path that he'd known would lead to heartbreak.

He just hadn't anticipated the rest of him shattering along with it.

Miller's palms wound to the back of his neck. "I swear, between you and Reagan, I'm going to be forced to take up heavy drinking again."

Towel lowering with his move, Deacon's head whipped to the side at the mention of her name. He didn't want to care, but unfortunately for him, feelings like the ones they shared didn't dissipate overnight.

"Is she okay?"

"I don't know." Miller's muscled shoulders lifted. "She's also having some kind of life crisis at the moment. Probably something to do with the mystery guy and moving."

Thanks to social media, Deacon was more than aware that Reagan had accepted a transfer to Chicago.

For someone who claimed to have a change of heart, Reagan didn't waste any time starting fresh.

Deacon eyes rolled to the ceiling. "Why am I not surprised?"

"I was. She was happy in Indianapolis until more recently." Miller's pointed stare fixed on Deacon's creased eyes. "Until you started Single in the City."

"A coincidence." Deacon wiped away beads of perspiration forming on his brow.

Miller's arms crossed. "And now that she's announced she's moving, you're getting in fights and playing like shit."

"Negative energy feeds on negative energy," Deacon said.

"No one else we know seems to be feeding off of that." Miller's lips pursed as he held Deacon's stare. "I'm fine. Kate's fine. Rin is also fine. Stella is Stella, but she's good. Rook, well, I haven't talked to him much lately, but as far as I know he's good too. Reggie still hates everything, but he always did, so no change there," Miller replied, cinching his arms tighter across his chest. "So forgive me if I have a hard time believing that you and Reagan going off the rails at the same time is a fluke."

"It's a free country. You can believe what you want."

Clicks sounded as Miller popped knuckles on each hand. "Why don't you tell me the truth and then I won't have to guess."

"There's nothing to tell," Deacon clipped.

He and Reagan were over.

Done.

He'd offered her everything and she said no. There was nothing more to the story.

Head cocking, Miller replied, "So you two aren't—"

"I can honestly say no." Deacon's lips dipped as his gaze dropped to the tile floor as their coach stormed into the locker room. His voice hushed to a raspy whisper. "Like I said. There's nothing to tell."

There was no epilogue to this story. No second edition soon to be released.

"I never thought I would say this to you," Miller snipped in a soft tone, "but I call bullshit. I can tell you're lying."

A flush darkened Deacon's browned skin.

When had Miller become so damn intuitive?

Deacon once fancied himself a fan of Kate, but now he wasn't so sure. No doubt, his best friend's new perceptiveness was her fault.

"I can prove I'm not lying," Deacon replied. "I'm going to see if Saachi wants to keep hanging out after the show wraps. And I wouldn't do that if Reagan and I were a thing, would I?"

He'd made the decision after Reagan's rejection.

The athlete had spent too much time focusing on a woman who didn't want him, when there was one who did standing right in front of him, so it was imperative that he start spending his time in a more worthwhile manner.

On paper, Saachi was his dream woman.

So now, all he had to do was convince his heart of the same thing.

Chapter Twenty-eight

"To victory." Deacon tipped his beer bottle to the center of the table, lifting his usual toast out of habit rather than celebration. "It was another close one, but we pulled it off."

Glass clanked as his teammates and friends joined in praising the Panther players for charting a win. Two more and their spot in the playoffs was secure.

Speckled with post game revelers, Lockerbie's buzzed with excitement, but Deacon couldn't muster the enthusiasm shared by the crowd.

His usually sharp game play had spiraled to a bungled mess.

His friendship with Miller was sparking with friction.

And Reagan's second absence from a home game did nothing to turn his poor mood around.

Sure, he'd said they were through, but he hadn't yet adapted to his new reality.

It was strange. Reagan not being in attendance at the stadium or their standard post-game outing. As frustrated as he was with her running away from what they could have been, Deacon missed seeing her. Talking to her.

Not that they'd ever been overly chatty in public. The two often kept space between themselves to avoid the impression that they could be anything more than friends.

But tonight, it was more than that.

For the first time in a long while, they wouldn't be pretending not to be an item. They wouldn't avoid each other to dodge suspicion.

Deacon's brow furrowed. Because her fears outweighed his love, they wouldn't be anything.

"You look like hell." Stella's palm patted Deacon's shoulder as she sat her cocktail glass on the table.

"I'm fine," Deacon snipped, even though he wasn't.

But the athlete wasn't going to broadcast that to the woman most likely to rub his face in his mistakes.

"Interesting take when you're wearing ten pounds of misery on your face despite a big win."

"I'm just tired." Deacon shrugged off her touch. "Thanks to you, I've had a lot going on lately."

Stella pushed her long, dark locks behind her shoulder. "Since I have some good news to share, I'm going to pretend like you didn't just use a crass tone with me."

"I don't need any more *good* news from you," Deacon scoffed. "You've given me quite enough already."

She was part of the reason he was in this mess in the first place.

"What's Stella giving you?" Miller chimed in.

"A headache," Deacon replied, fingers circling his temple.

Miller lifted a bottle to his lips as his forehead lifted. "I remember the feeling."

Deacon looked up to Miller's towering form. The athlete never wished ill on his best friend, but a part of him missed the days when Miller was a mess and Deacon was the one who had it together.

"Any chance you want to go rogue again so she won't have time for the rest of us?"

Kate looped around Miller's arm, melting into his black t-shirt. "Not a chance, Deacon. Don't even put that idea into the world."

"I'll second that," Stella said, turning to Deacon and rubbing her palms together. "Save the doom and gloom for yourself, Bailey. Tonight, we're celebrating."

Celebrating? How was he supposed to happy when his whole life was crumbling to pieces?

"So what's your big news?" Kate asked, reminding her friend they were all awaiting her announcement.

"Ahh, it's very exciting." A sly smile spread on Stella's red painted lips. "A reporter from the paper accidentally leaked information about tomorrow's local section, and I'm dying to share it with everyone."

Kate's knowing stare bored into Stella. "Did he *accidentally* share? Or did you force his hand?"

"If he didn't want me to know, then he should have had a stronger resolve," Stella snipped as her shoulders lifted. "It's not my fault he has no spine."

"Poor guy didn't stand a chance," Kate said with a sigh, resting her head on Miller's chest.

"Poor me," Deacon replied, taking a swig from his bottle. "All of her *fun* updates seem to be about me lately."

"You say that like it's a bad thing," Rook chimed in from across the table. His bare arms leaned into the dilapidated slab. "You don't know how lucky you are to have the attention."

"You'll change your mind about that someday when you're the one under her thumb." Deacon's fingers formed a fake gun and fired at the youngest player's chest. "Besides, I've already got enough of the spotlight. I don't need anymore."

"You could show a little gratitude for all of my time and effort," Stella snipped.

"Do I have to appreciate attention I didn't want?" Deacon protested.

"Actually—"

"Forget it," Deacon cut in, ending Stella's pending rant as his hands wiped down his face. "Just spill it already, and let us know who's up to bat now."

"With pleasure." With the glow of triumph shining in her eyes, Stella clapped her hands to capture the crowd's attention.

Used to Stella's commands, heads turned without hesitation at her call.

"Everyone, listen up. This evening's celebration isn't just about the Panthers win. Tonight, we raise our glasses in honor of our very own Miller Cassidy, our beloved teammate, and the man the city of Indianapolis just announced as this year's Champion of Character!"

Applause erupted as Deacon's body swayed under the swift force of bodies moving in to congratulate Miller with pats on the back and high fives.

Deacon blinked a hard double as he regained his balance and focus.

Had he heard Stella correctly? Miller was the winner? For a character award?

The Champion of Character award was one of the city's most prestigious accolades. Given to those who exemplified excellence in their field. To a Hoosier who was philanthropic, motivating, and giving.

Any other year, Deacon would have been thrilled to see his friend recognized for his dedication to the Donor Foundation. Would have donned his tuxedo with pride and schmoozed with the city's elite while sipping champagne and beaming a radiant smile in support of his good friend.

But this year? It was obvious the universe was taunting him. Reminding Deacon that he'd abandoned his morals while spending the better part of a year lying to his best friend. Pining for his sister.

And for what? For the relationship to turn to dust?

While Deacon was distracted with chasing Reagan, Miller had turned into an upstanding citizen, and Deacon had become . . . *what had he become?*

Chapter Twenty-nine

FIFTY of the city's red, white, and blue flags lined the hallway leading to the Marriott's largest banquet hall. A hum of chatter spread about the large space as hundreds of Indianapolis' elite gathered to honor the success of local businesses and citizens. Crisp navy linens adorned the tables while red and white flowers popped from the simple cylinder vases placed in the center.

Reagan smoothed the front of her black dress as she, Miller, and Kate wandered through the crowd and toward the front stage. The mock turtle neck collar hugging her neck was beautiful in theory, but its suffocating tightness did nothing to ease Reagan's anxiety.

It'd been a week since Deacon had proposed, and she'd turned him down. Though her heart felt the pangs like it happened yesterday.

Despite the turmoil between them, there was no doubt the athlete would be present this evening. As Miller's best friend, and a teammate, his attendance was all but mandatory.

And, thanks to the Single Series, he wouldn't be alone.

Winding an arm behind Kate's back, Miller scanned the crowded space. "Let's go find our table so we know where it is and you ladies can put your sweaters down."

"You just want to be able to switch a chocolate cake to your place setting before anyone notices," Kate said, bumping her hip to Miller's.

"The other option appears to be carrot cake which is offensive to all decent desserts," Miller replied. The athlete sent a puny stare down to his girlfriend. "And I wouldn't have to plot ahead of time if you would agree to trade me just this once."

"I love you, but not that much," Kate teased.

Miller pinched her waist with playful mirth. "Just when I was starting to think you could be the one. I'm wounded."

"Would a kiss help you heal?" Kate's fingers wrapped his chin and pulled his lips to hers.

"It's a place to start," Miller grinned, looping his arms around her back and holding her firmly against his body as he sank into another long drag from her mouth.

"Uhh . . . while you two are dealing with that important matter, I'm going to hit the bar," Reagan said, looking for an excuse to escape the smitten couple's side.

Kai hadn't exaggerated their hands on relationship.

"Can I bring you back anything?"

"I'll take white wine," Kate said, not tearing her stare from her boyfriend.

"Water," Miller replied.

Reagan's floor length skirt swished at her feet as she wandered toward the bar. Dodging through the small crowd gathered round, she sighed with relief as her arms met the lifted counter. "I'll take two reislings, a water, and do you have any straight liquor for shots?"

She needed something to calm her nerves before she spoke to Deacon, who she was sure she'd bump into any moment. He was a stickler for being on time, and according to the invitation, the cocktail hour started fifteen minutes prior.

"Sounds like someone is here to party," a familiar male voice chuckled. "But I'm not sure this is that kind of place."

Reagan's head whipped as her eyes took in the gorgeous face smiling in her direction.

"Chase. What are you doing here?"

"Don't think I'm worthy of the honor?" The firefighter's fingers brushed the five o'clock shadow dusting his chiseled jawline as a cocky twinkle sparkled in his green eyes.

The tilt of his lips oozed a sauciness that confirmed why women across the city threw themselves at the gentleman.

Once upon a time, this obvious rogue would have been exactly Reagan's type, and she would have swooned at his wolfish gaze.

How much simpler her life would be if she were still that girl.

"I didn't say you're not deserving," Reagan replied, pushing a ten into the tip jar. "I just didn't expect to see you here. That's all."

"The calendar crew always attends to support the Hearts on Fire Foundation. We're up for several awards." Muscles bulged against the slim cut of his dark suit as he smoothed his black tie. "I hear your brother is up for an award as well."

"Surprisingly so." Reagan chuckled. "Who would have thought? Miller Cassidy . . . from hellion to honorary."

"Where is your dear brother hiding tonight?" Chase's eyes scanned the room as he leaned toward Reagan. "And is he going to pummel me if I help you carry those drinks back to your table? I'm not one of his favorite people."

"He's matured a lot in the last few months, so I'm sure it will be fine as long as you don't instigate something." Reagan handed him Miller's beer as she wound her fingers around the stems of the wine glasses. "And if you do, I'll throttle you myself."

"If you're going to make a threat, my dear, you have to make it sound less appealing." Chase sipped from his cocktail as his eyes took in her figure. "A throttling from you could be fun. Especially in that dress."

"No such luck today," Reagan clipped as she began the route back to their assigned table. "The gown belongs to Rin, and I'm taking a break from men."

"Sounds like you're singing the sad song of heartbreak," Chase said.

Reagan's shoulder lifted. "Maybe."

"That would explain why you never called me back after our date."

"Maybe I just wasn't interested," Reagan said. "I'm sure there are some women you can't sweep off their feet.

"Unlikely, but I suppose there's always an outlier." Chase's brow wrinkled. "Who's the guy?"

"Does it matter?"

Chase's head bobbled. "Could I take him? I do love a good competition."

Reagan took in Chase's muscular build. His bulk was thicker than Deacon's, but that was to be expected from a firefighter. His form was made to move and lift falling objects, whereas Deacon was built to soar from one edge of the court to the other.

"You're bigger, but he'd be faster," Reagan said with a slight grin. "Even if you could land a sucker punch, you'd still lose."

"I see," Chase said, allowing Reagan to step ahead of him as their path between two groups narrowed. He bent to her ear. "You've borrowed more than Rin's dress. You took a pair of her love goggles, as well."

"I had my own," Reagan said, looking back to the firefighter. "But it doesn't matter now. He and I . . . it's not going to work out."

Chase's head tilted with intrigue. "Can I ask why?"

"It's complicated," Reagan said.

"See, that's what everyone always says. *It's complicated.* But I guess I imagine that if I ever loved someone that much, that it wouldn't be complicated at all. That I'd do whatever was necessary to be with them. Even if it meant swallowing my pride."

"Easier said than done," Reagan replied.

"But wouldn't it better to be rejected than to always wonder what if? I feel like those two words could eat at a person's sanity forever."

Was Chase right? If Reagan left for Chicago without laying all of her cards out on the table one more time, would she always question what could have been?

Weaving through the scattering of people, tables, and chairs, Reagan continued to their assigned table.

When Reagan arrived at table four, she found the arrangement different than anticipated. Instead of the Panther's head coach and his wife, who were happily chatting two tables away, Deacon and his date were placing their drinks in front of their plates.

A hard swallow ran down Reagan's throat. As if the encounter wasn't awkward enough, two camera lenses were trained on their every move.

Before she could speak, Kate swept over and relieved Reagan of both wine glasses while a whisper escaped her lips. "I swear I didn't know they were at our table, or I would have warned you."

Deacon's rigid glare didn't indicate surprise at the placement, yet it was far from welcoming. "Reagan."

"*Deacon,*" Reagan clipped, unable to hide her jealousy of the woman now clinging to his arm. Saachi was draped in a form fitting, stunning black silk that reminded her of the cloak of midnight covering a country sky.

And Deacon was equally dapper in his suit. The quirky, black and white, small print hounds tooth was her favorite. It capped his muscled shoulders in exactly the right place, and the trim cut of the coat highlighted his athletic figure. She'd mentioned her fondness for the piece on several occasions, so the fact that Deacon wore it for an evening out with Saachi wasn't lost on Reagan. He'd wanted to impress his date.

Chase wrapped his arm around her back and leaned into her ear with a whisper. "This wouldn't by chance be . . ."

"Yeah," she rasped.

Had her reaction to Deacon's date been that obvious?

Chase's eyes floated toward Saachi. "Oh, so this is . . ."

"Bad," Reagan replied. "Very bad."

"YOU'RE NOT USUALLY one for formal affairs," Deacon said, shoving his hands in his pants pockets.

Decked out in flowing, navy chiffon, that tied at her neck, Reagan emitted an effortless sophistication that reminded Deacon of models in perfume commercials. Soft waves of auburn curls framed her stoic face, draping over her keyhole back.

The back where Chase freaking Howard was resting his hand and whispering sweet nothings into her ear.

Who the hell did this guy think he was taking such a familiar stance with her? They'd been on what, one date?

A hard swallow ran down Deacon's throat as he surveyed their sense of ease with each other.

Was it possible they'd been on more? Was that why she rejected his proposal? For Chase?

Noting his interest in her date, Reagan's cutting gaze wandered to Saachi. "You're usually not one for casual affairs, but I guess we're all making an exception this evening."

Deacon's teeth ground. Was she seriously calling him out for attending with Saachi while the cameras were rolling? When she had Howard dangling by her side?

The firefighter's cockiness seeped from his pores and his dark, spikey hair oozed frat boy, asshole.

Surely, she didn't find him appealing?

"This is Chase Howard," Reagan said, wrapping his arm with her hand. "He works for Indy Fire, and he's Mr. October in this year's Hearts on Fire calendar."

"Yeah." A huff sounded from Deacon's chest. "We've met."

He had more to say on the subject, but none of the words floating about his head were appropriate for public expression. Not with cameras hovering.

Beyond having a few run ins with Chase's crew at Lockerbie's, he'd heard Rin rattle on about her monthly segments featuring Indy Fire's hot shots. Her stories painted them as unsophisticated and immature.

Of course, Reagan would find that appealing. A man like Chase wasn't looking to settle down. He was only looking for—

Deacon's stomach clenched as did his grip on his drink. Jealousy boiled as the athlete thought about what it was the heathen was after.

"Nice to see you again, Howard," Miller said, shaking the newcomer's hand before gesturing across the table.

"It is?" Chase's face puzzled.

"Of course," Miller said, gesturing to the woman at his side. "My girlfriend, Kate, you know Deacon, and this is his soon to be girlfriend, Saachi."

Reagan's blue eyes ballooned as she took a step backward. "I'm sorry. *Girlfriend?*"

Deacon's lids sank as his stomach plummeted to his feet.

What the hell was Miller doing calling Saachi his girlfriend? Did no one with the last name Cassidy see the cameras surrounding them?

Plus, Deacon hadn't fully meant the statement that was fueling Miller's assumption. He'd made an off the cuff comment in the locker room to get his friend off his back. The athlete hadn't actually decided what he was going to do about Saachi.

She'd been more than understanding about his hang up with Reagan, and in theory, she was his perfect match. But perfect on paper didn't always play out the same in reality.

Not that reality always played out well either. He and Reagan had shared an undeniable spark. Hell, a whole fire.

But the flames hadn't been enough to burn away the hurt from Reagan's past, so now she had to live with the future she'd created.

One without him.

"The show still has another segment to go, but . . ." Saachi began, resting her free hand on Deacon's forearm.

Deacon's hand fell over his date's and hushed her words. "We don't owe Reagan an explanation."

"Of course, not." Reagan snipped, kicking at her skirt. "It's your choice if you want to make a rushed decision."

Deacon's head shook. Stubborn to her core, Reagan wasn't going to let the conversation drop peacefully. She was going to send them all spiraling into the flames of Miller's fury when he put two and two together.

Then again, if Reagan no longer cared about Miller finding out, why should he?

Hell, he'd wanted to tell his friend the truth from the beginning, and what was there even to tell now? That they were nothing?

"It's been several weeks, so I'm not sure I'd say they've rushed it," Miller replied, a wrinkle forming on his forehead. "Not everyone takes things as slow as you, Rea."

As Reagan's gaze drifted to her date, Chase's arm looped around her back as if he were comforting her. As if their relationship were at a level where he felt compelled to do so.

"*Perhaps* some people just need time to sort out their feelings,"

Reagan argued, her eyes shifting back to the conversation.

"Those who have feelings," Deacon clipped.

It wasn't his finest moment, but seriously, had she even waited five minutes after they broke up to take up with Chase? The annoying pest who was whispering in her ear again.

Reagan's mouth gaped as she pulled her wine glass to her chest. "Are you implying that I don't?"

"I know this will be shocking for you to learn, but not everything is about *you*, Reagan."

"Yes, thanks to my father I've known that for quite some time," Reagan said, turning to her new friend as she tugged at her turtleneck top. "Chase, will you accompany me to the lobby? It's rather stifling in here at the moment."

"Of course." Chase placed his hand on Reagan's lower back. "Lead the way, my lady."

His lady? *His* lady?

When had she become someone he felt he had possession of?

"She's not leaving with you," Deacon snipped, clasping Reagan's arm and halting her movement. "If she needs an escort, one of us will take care of it."

"I think you've done enough this evening," Chase returned, tugging Reagan his direction.

Deacon took a step closer to the stranger and met him with a glaring eye. His hand pushed against Chase's crisp shirt. "You don't know anything about this situation, so I suggest you stay out of it."

"He's fine, Deac. Just let it go," Miller interjected.

"Exactly. I'm trying to stay out of it," Chase replied, swatting Deacon's hand away. "By leaving. With Reagan."

Deacon used both hands to shove at Chase's chest, causing the bounder to stumble backwards. "She's not going anywhere with you, asshole."

"Chill out." Miller held a palm to Deacon's shirt as he nodded to the closest. "This is not the place."

It wasn't the place. It wasn't the time. Deacon was growing tired of waiting for things to be right.

"Like you have room to judge," Deacon said, shirking Miller's touch as Chase restored his stance.

"I'm the asshole?" Back on his feet, Chase straightened his tie. "Who is starting a scene at a charity banquet?"

"I'm protecting a friend," Deacon growled as Miller pushed him back once more.

"One who doesn't need protection," Reagan said, attempting to corral the firefighter as he stepped closer to the athlete. However, Chase swiftly stepped in front of her.

"Stay over there. I deal with out of control people all the time." Chase edged Reagan to the side.

Catching on her train, Reagan's heel wobbled, causing her to tumble into a nearby chair. Forgetting Deacon, Miller was by her side in a second flat, helping her to her feet.

Deacon's eyes lit with red fury. "Did you push her?"

Chase's face paled at his blunder. "I was just trying to get her out of the way."

"I knew you were an asshole," Deacon growled. Cocking his elbow, he sent a stiff fist flying toward the interloper.

Ducking with unexpected speed, Chase dipped below Deacon's fist. Still, Deacon heard the swift crack of connection.

A rumble of chaos erupted as shouts echoed about the banquet hall.

"What the hell is wrong with you?" Reagan shouted as she collapsed to the floor, hovering over a folded form.

It was only then that Deacon saw his victim.

Sprawled on the floor with blood dripping down his chin and shirt was Miller.

The person they'd been trying to protect for months.

♥

HOW HAD THIS HAPPENED again? Reagan's hands fluttered over Miller's crumpled form. She gave up a shot at happiness in exchange for her brother's wellbeing, and he'd ended up bleeding on the floor anyways.

She was damned if she did, and damned if she didn't.

Reagan watched as Deacon turned on his heel, his dark jacket fading into the crowd as he stormed out of the banquet hall. With steam rolling off his head, no one dared to follow the disgruntled athlete. Not even the camera crew.

Instead, a flurry of people descended over Miller, offering him napkins, ice, and water while Kate helped him into a chair.

Jumping into action, Chase pushed the blathering onlookers back, with the exception of Kate, who hovered over his shoulder. Wadding a cloth under Miller's dripping nose, the firefighter urged him to lean forward. Reagan's brother's green eyes narrowed with irritation, but he followed the instructions without argument.

Still, Miller's eyes diverted when Reagan sent him an apologetic glance.

"I knew it," he mumbled.

"What?" Reagan chewed at her lip.

Miller's sharp gaze cut back to her own. "How long?"

"How long, what?" Reagan questioned, though she knew good and well what he was asking.

"Don't make me say it," Miller cut. "You know exactly what I mean."

A heavy breath flowed from Reagan's lips. "A few months."

"Define a few."

Reagan's eyes clinched as her face scrunched. "Nine-ish."

"What the hell? Nine? That's almost an entire year." Miller's fingers combed through his blonde locks.

"Well," Reagan replied, "you know what they say about time flying."

The somber stare on Miller's face indicated that he didn't appreciate her cheeky answer.

Luckily, Reagan was saved from further inquiries when Stella made her way over to the scene, shooing people away with her approach.

"We're all done here. Go on about your evening," she dictated to those still waiting in the wings. "This is a team matter."

Her tone was even, but her severe stare demanded the crowd dissipate.

Once their small group was no longer under the scrutiny of watchful bystanders, Stella's short train whipped with her body as she turned to those assembled. Her words clipped at the tension in the air. "Anyone care to explain what happened?"

Lips pursed as eyes darted to the ground. Hands found their way to pockets and fiddled with clutches.

Stella scanned the dropped stares as her stilettos carried her forward. Her dark brow lifted as she surveyed the group. "I'm not surprised to find that Cassidy is involved, but he didn't do this by himself. Who is the other perpetrator?"

Her question was met with stressed silence. Eyes diverted to the ceiling as nervous coughs sounded.

"There are cameras for crying out loud. It's not like I can't find out," Stella snipped. Pausing in front of the rookie, Stella's fingers raised his chin, and forced him to meet her gaze. "Who?"

"Deac," the rookie mumbled.

"I see." Stella's head shook as she turned to Reagan. Her pointed finger placing warranted accusations. "What did I tell you? I knew this would end in disaster."

"You knew about them? How could you know and not tell me?" Miller hissed as he attempted to stand, but Stella shoved his shoulders back down before the athlete could find his footing.

"Oh, come on. You knew." Stella's bare arms opened to the group. "Everyone knew."

All around, heads began to bob in agreement and Reagan's cheeks flushed a deep shade of scarlet.

Everyone knew.

All these months she and Deacon had been trying to hide their interest, and for what?

For everyone to know anyways.

For Miller to end up laid out on the floor with a bleeding nose.

In trying to prevent hurt, Reagan and Deacon had created more.

After a minute of applying pressure to slow the bleed, Chase pulled the cloth napkin away to assess the damage. Angling Miller's chin to one side and then the other, he studied the athlete's hardened face.

"I don't think it's broken, but you probably want to get checked out by a doctor just to be sure. I'll make a call to the emergency room over at Methodist and see if they can sneak you in a back door."

"Thank you," Reagan replied.

Chase's hands dropped to his side as his gaze shifted to Reagan. "I'll leave you all be for now. You can find me in the lobby when you're ready to go, but don't hesitate to get me sooner if you need something."

"We'll be fine until then," Reagan said, sliding into the seat beside Miller. Her eyes pleading for his forgiveness. "Won't we?"

"Maybe when my face stops throbbing," Miller whined.

Kate's eyes scanned the brother and sister scene unfolding and quickly excused herself after popping a kiss to Miller's purpling cheek.

"I think I'll go get fresh ice. I'll be back in a minute."

"Good idea." Miller winced as his fingers tapped his nose.

"It's not the first time you've been scraped up," Reagan said as she watched Kate move for the exit. "You'll heal."

"My face, yes. My trust . . . that's debatable."

"You have to know, the last thing I wanted to do was hurt you. In fact, this whole scene was the climax of emotions built from trying to protect you."

"And look what good that did," Miller scoffed.

"I know," Reagan's lids lowered. "Deacon wanted to tell you the truth, and I wouldn't let him. It's my fault this happened."

"You're actually admitting that you were wrong?" Miller's brow wrinkled.

Reagan nodded. "I know it's hard for you to see, but I've grown up, Miller. I'm not a little girl anymore."

"But you're still my little sister."

"And I always will be, but I have to live my own life. Make my own choices and mistakes. Big mistakes in this case."

"We all played our part," Miller said, readjusting his ice pack. "I didn't handle the Brandon thing well back in college, so I suppose you were justified in assuming I wouldn't be a fan of you dating yet another one of my friends."

"Us being together . . . it didn't seem worth rocking your newfound calm," Reagan said.

A heavy sigh sounded from Miller's chest. "I appreciate the sentiment, but I'm not the same person I was back then. I've changed, too, and I thought you, of all people, knew that."

"I'm really sorry, Miller. I wish we'd handled it differently, but we did what seemed right at the time. I never meant to betray your trust or go behind your back."

"You didn't tell me the truth, but I'm not sure you went behind my back," Miller said, tugging at his reddened ear. "Stella was right. It was rather obvious there was something going on between the two of you."

"I guess we weren't as secretive as we imagined."

"Because you can't hide love," Miller said, tilting his head in assessment. "And you love him, don't you?"

Reagan's lips pursed as her head nodded. "Not that it matters now. I never told him, and he's with Saachi. You said it yourself."

"Yet he didn't get in a fight over her, did he?" Miller's arms crossed his bloodied shirt.

"No," Reagan replied, her hand fiddling with the collar wrapped around her neck. "But I have to let him go."

"Why?"

"Because he deserves more than me. I'm a flight risk like Dad. I'm no good for him. For anybody."

"He said that?" Miller's eyes widened.

"No, but I know it's true. I've always been so worried about being the one who gets hurt, that I couldn't see how I was hurting others."

"And you did a lot of damage this time?"

Reagan nodded. "More than a little."

Miller's head wavered. "Then sweep up your mess."

"But—"

"No buts, Reagan." Miller held up his hand to silence her words. "For the first time, don't let this be about anyone else. You can choose to fix your mistake, or you can choose to deal with it, but either way, it's on *you.*"

Miller lifted from his seat as she swallowed his harsh truth.

He wasn't standing in their way. Nor was Saachi.

Reagan Cassidy had built the fence which held her back from finding true happiness.

But how did one destroy a barrier they'd spent years fortifying?

Chapter Thirty

STARING over the rim of his lowball tumbler, Deacon's head shook as he watched the hotel's bar tender rattle and pour a yellow tinged liquid into a martini glass, topping the rim with a lemon.

The fool.

Martinis were infinitely better when stirred.

Unlike life. Which was superior when it wasn't shaken or stirred. It was best when poured straight from the bottle like the aged whiskey swirling in his glass. His third of the night. Because . . . well, because why not?

He'd lost the girl.

He'd punched his best friend.

Sacchi had left without a peep.

Then, Stella had scorched him with all the words Saachi left unsaid.

Deacon's once organized life was in shambles. Because Reagan was right. Love ruined everything.

"Ahem."

Deacon didn't turn to the clearing throat.

If the overwhelming spice of Miller's cologne hadn't given him away, his towering shadow would have. Deacon could feel his friend's sharp gaze cutting at his neck, boring a thousand pounds of tension on the athlete's shoulders.

"I promise I'll let you pummel me in a minute, but I'd really appreciate it if I could finish my drink first." Deacon took a slow drag of the dark liquid, enjoying the burn that radiated down his esophagus.

A thud sounded as Miller sank onto the backless barstool beside him.

"I should send you sailing into July for punching me and doing who knows what to my sister," Miller said, draping his coat on the counter. "But Kate said I should hear your side of the story before I make any rash decisions."

"I'd rather you just knock me out," Deacon said, setting the glass on the marble bar top as the faint hum of jazz swirled around them.

Miller's fingers drummed against the counter. "Do you want to tell me what happened?"

Deacon's torso shifted to his friend. A purplish green bruise sat on Miller's cheek. A noted lack of white bandages indicated that while his nose was slightly swollen, it probably wasn't broken. That was the only positive Deacon could find in the evening. At least he hadn't taken Miller out of the playoffs.

"I'd rather not talk about it."

"Well, I'd like to hear about it, so why don't you tell me anyways." Miller's elbows leaned into the counter. "And start at the beginning."

Deacon drank in a deep breath. Possibly his last for a while. Miller would surely break several of his ribs.

Lifting his glass, Deacon flagged the bartender's attention. "Another for my friend."

While alcohol wouldn't drown Miller's anger, perhaps it would dull his coming rage to a frenzy rather than fury.

A sigh filtered from Miller's lips. "That bad, huh?"

"Worse," Deacon said, pushing the fresh glass in front of his friend. He took a sip from his tumbler before adding, "Her summer party. That's where it all started."

"I sent you there to comfort her, not ... not ... you know." Miller's knuckles went white as he clutched his glass, but he didn't move from his seat.

"And I did. Help her. As a friend. Only friends. But then ..." Deacon's head tilted to the side, hoping the gesture indicated the words he couldn't say.

Miller's scowl deepened. "You took it up a notch."

"We'd both been fighting it for months. Pretending that there was nothing there because we wanted to do right by you. But that night, she tripped walking out of the elevator, and the moment we touched ... it was unstoppable." The athlete looked to his friend. "Perhaps you can relate?"

"I've known a similar force," Miller said, his gaze focused on the amber liquid swirling in his glass. "But our situations are not the same because I didn't lie about my newfound feelings."

"I wanted to tell you," Deacon said, his lashes lowering. "But I didn't know how you'd react, and my desire to be with Reagan blinded my sense of reason, so I went along with her plan to keep it a secret."

"I'd say," Miller scoffed. "You let a hook up come between our friendship."

"I can't deny that our physical connection is off the charts. Almost unreal—"

"No," Miller cut as his flattened palm lifted. "No. No. No."

"I was going to say that it's more than that," Deacon defended. "Reagan has passion by the pounds, and that fierce, Cassidy personality I've come to appreciate. She's protective of those she cares for."

"She is loyal to a fault," Miller agreed.

"Yeah." Deacon's finger traced the rim of his glass. "Which is why . . . I . . ." A slow exhale escaped the athlete's lips. "I love her."

Miller's eyes cinched shut, but his head nodded with understanding. "I'm guessing you told her so, and she freaked out?"

"I did worse than that." Deacon chuckled. "I asked her to marry me."

Miller's eyes bugged as his mouth gaped, closed, and then opened again. "You did what?"

"I proposed. Marriage."

"Marriage?" Miller's lashes beat a hard double as he processed Deacon's words. "I suspected something was going on between you. I mean, you two haven't exactly been subtle lately. But that—I didn't expect to hear that. I thought you were just hooking up. I don't even know what to say about a proposal."

"Don't worry, there's no response necessary," Deacon replied, waving off Miller's concern. "She said no."

"I assumed as much," Miller said, taking swig from his tumbler. "Reagan has had a jaded view of commitment since the day my dad walked out the door."

"I'm aware." Deacon polished off the last quarter inch of whiskey.

Miller's face softened. "I'm sorry, man. I wasn't trying to rub it in your face."

"You have nothing to apologize for. I'm the one who is sorry." Deacon pushed his shirt sleeves above his elbows. "For so many things."

"Deac—"

"Don't try to make it better. I don't deserve it." Deacon's long limbs lifted from the stool. "Let's get to the thrashing. I'd like nothing more than to forget this evening. The week even, if you can manage it."

Miller's seat swiveled to the side as he looked up to his friend. "A few punches won't make you forget her."

"I have to try something," Deacon said, lifting his suit coat from the adjacent seat. "And I don't know what else to do."

"I don't think there's anything else you can do," Miller said, lifting to his feet. "I think you have to let her go."

"You didn't let Kate go."

"That was different. I missed the telethon and..." Understanding dawned on Miller's face. "I missed the telethon because of you, didn't I? You were the one I saw in the hallway. That's why you ran."

A grimace grew on Deacon's face as he gave a slight nod.

"Maybe I should knock you out." The sleeves on Miller's dress shirt crinkled as he pushed the cuffs up to the crook of his elbows. "Then again, maybe Reagan has done enough damage in the name of the Cassidy family."

"I deserve it," Deacon said. "For lying, and deceiving, and for being a shitty friend."

"You'd only be a shitty friend if you did wrong by her," Miller said. "You can't help that she has a twisted view on relationships."

"I wanted to be the one to change her mind," Deacon said. "I thought it could be different with us."

"You can't change people, Deacon. They have to want it for themselves." Miller said, lifting from his seat. "Reagan won't let anyone else fight for her love until she realizes it's something worth fighting for."

"So I just let her leave?"

"Yeah," Miller clapped a hand on Deacon's shoulder. "We all do."

Chapter Thirty-one

STROLLING into the lobby at Penn Tower after running Sunday morning errands, Reagan waved at the white haired doorman. "Afternoon, Lou."

"Miss Cassidy." Lou's head dipped in greeting as he reached for a medium sized box and placed it on the counter. "A package arrived for you a little bit ago."

Beyond a weekend distribution, the shiny, silver wrapping indicated that the box wasn't an average delivery. However, Reagan couldn't recall placing an order from the type of store that would send such an elaborate bundle.

"You're sure it's for me?"

Lou's hand flattened his dark tie. "Positive."

"Who's it from?" Reagan's fingers toyed with the purple bow tied atop the parcel.

"Mr. Bailey dropped it off. I was given instructions to hand it to you personally." A smile grew on Lou's lips as his elbows leaned into the high counter. "Must be something special."

"I suppose we'll find out," Reagan said, her heart thumping as she pulled the box to her chest. "Thank you."

"You're welcome. Have a nice day, ma'am." Lou waved as Reagan made her way to the elevator. With the tap of her fingers, the circular up button lit with a pale glow.

On the ride up, Reagan couldn't peel her eyes from the box. And not because the iridescent wrapping was eye catching.

Deacon sent her a gift.

But why?

They hadn't spoken since the incident in the banquet hall.

Was it an apology? An attempt at reconciling?

And what gift conveyed those messages?

Reagan desperately wanted to find out, but the lift was crawling at a speed that made turtles look fast. How had she never noticed the elevator was so slow?

What felt like an hour later, when the metal doors cracked, Reagan had her silver key ready. Flipping the lock, she scrambled into the apartment, dropping her purse and keys to the floor with a clatter.

Perched on the couch with heads turned and eyes as wide as deer caught on the side of the street, Kate, Stella, and Rin watched her fumble with the package.

"What's going on?" Kate asked.

Reagan dropped the silver box on the wide counter that separated the living room from the kitchen. "Deacon sent me a gift."

It was strange, making such a declaration without first checking to see if Miller was home. But now that her brother knew the truth about their past romantic connection, there was no point in keeping the grantor's name a secret.

Rin pushed her knees and hovered over the back of the leather couch. "What is it?"

Ribbon fluttered to the counter as Reagan's fingers pulled at the loose bow. "I have no idea."

Eight eyes studied the box with inquisitive contemplation.

"It's too big to be jewelry," Stella said, fiddling with the turquoise ring wrapped around her middle finger as she strolled to Reagan's side. "Which is truly disappointing considering Deacon's income. He could throw some serious stones your direction."

"I don't care what it is. I'm more worried about what it means," Reagan replied.

"Maybe he's trying to say he's sorry," Kate said, folding a leg under the other as she sat on the table.

"What does Deacon have to be sorry for?" Stella questioned.

"He punched Miller," Kate said.

"Exactly," Stella scoffed. "So he should be sending Miller something nice, not Reagan."

"She's right." Reagan glanced over her shoulder and met Kate's curious gaze. "Maybe he's trying to say goodbye."

"Only one way to find out," Kate said, patting the top of the box.

With the excitement of a six year old on Christmas morning, the flight attendant tore through the crisp wrapping paper. She was greeted by a navy and yellow box that was decorated with Indiana's state flag.

Stella's brow wrinkled. "Interesting choice of packaging."

"What's in it?" Rin questioned, joining the group around the mysterious box.

Reagan popped the lid, her fingers flipping through the assortment of goods layered inside. "A Colts shirt, Tell City Pretzels, a Sun King beer, St. Elmo's cocktail sauce."

"What the hell kind of gift is this?" Stella scoffed, reaching for the cocktail sauce. She flipped the bottle upside down as if that might reveal a hidden secret. "A Super Bowl party bag? I imagined Deacon to be a bit more of a romantic."

Eyes creasing, Kate picked up a box of popcorn and surveyed the label. "I don't think it's about football. That wouldn't make any sense. Unless you two have an inside joke about stadium food?"

"This isn't stadium food." Rin picked up a jar of apple butter and nodded with understanding. "These are all Indiana classics."

"A going away gift of all the things I won't have easy access to in Chicago," Reagan's shoulders dropped as her lids blinked back the drops hovering on the rims of her eyes.

"So it is kind of romantic." A gentle smile curved on Kate's lips. "Only Deacon would be this thoughtful."

"It's not a kind gesture." Reagan's throat tightened as her head snapped toward her brother's girlfriend. "It's a sign he wants me to leave."

Rin's palm wrapped Reagan's forearm in a sign of care. "Maybe he just wants to support your decision."

"Or he wants me out of the way," Reagan countered.

She'd tried to push Deacon out of her life, but he'd never budged. Not while her feelings wavered. But now . . . now that Reagan knew she loved him. Understood what it meant to be without him. Now, Deacon caved and stepped to the side.

"Despite my best efforts, I don't think he's wishing you away." Stella tossed the cocktail sauce back in the box and wiped her hands clean of imaginary dust. "Did you see the punch he laid on Miller the other night when he thought he was swinging at Chase? That was not an indifferent tap."

Reagan flopped into the upholstered chair positioned at the head of the table. "Then why hasn't he sought me out?"

Rin's lips pursed as she glanced down at Reagan's slumped form. "Maybe he's waiting for you to pursue him this time? You did reject his proposal."

Her friend was right. Deacon was more understanding than the average person, but he had pride to maintain and a heart to protect. And Reagan couldn't blame the athlete for shielding himself from her. It was a natural reaction for those burned by love's flames. A response she knew all too well.

And such a level of hurt wasn't easily forgotten. Or forgiven.

For anyone.

Reagan's wretched face fell to her palms. "What am I going to do?"

"Do you love him?" Kate asked, brushing her hand over Reagan's red locks.

A single tear ran down Reagan's cheek. "I do."

"Then you have to tell him," Rin said, leaning her hip to the table.

"What if that's not enough?" Reagan's sorrowful stare met her friend's gazes. "What if he doesn't believe me?"

"Then you'll show him," Stella said, cocking a confident hand on her hip. "No more waiting for the universe to give a sign. Be the sign."

"Be the sign," Reagan repeated, her shaky voice lacking Stella's conviction. "But how?"

A sly smile lifted on Stella's lips. "I might have a plan."

Chapter Thirty-two

"**I** CAN'T believe this is it," Deacon said, buttoning his navy suit coat while scanning the auditorium from the right wing. "The last night."

A hum of excitement buzzed through the antique theater as murmuring audience members awaited the start of the finale, leaving Deacon wishing his enthusiasm matched theirs. But ever since Reagan had announced she was moving to Chicago, it was hard for him to muster emotion beyond melancholy indifference.

Deacon didn't particularly care for the fact that she'd declined his proposal either, but at least that hadn't been a complete surprise. He'd known for years she didn't believe in the age old sacrament.

Even so, he'd assumed she'd still be in a place where he stood a chance at changing her mind in the future.

But with the mention of Chicago, she'd made her intentions clear and dashed all of Deacon's dreams of reconciling.

It had been a harsh reality to accept. That he couldn't make her stay. But Miller was right. He had to let her go. It was the only way.

"It's also the big night where you're finally in control," Rin said, smoothing down her ruby dress. The satin shone under the soft glow of overhead lights. "Thus far, the audience has been picking dates for you, but now you get to choose if you want to continue seeing one of them outside the confines of the show."

"A few weeks ago, I wasn't sure what I was going to do in this moment, but now . . ." Deacon's hands found his pockets. "I suppose the answer is clear but not in the way I expected."

Deacon had once imagined he'd make Reagan jealous and she'd come to see her true feelings. See that he was worth taking a risk.

In truth, he'd succeeded half way. Reagan had grown envious of Saachi and her relationship with Deacon, but it never advanced to anything more than that. Reagan had never progressed to a mad profession of love at the thought of losing him.

Instead, she'd taken a job transfer to Chicago and blown out the final candle on their cake. Now, all that remained was smoke from the many fires that had once burned between them.

"So do you know what you're going to do?" Rin asked, rubbing in the gloss on her lips as she adjusted the lapel mic attached to her square neckline.

"Yeah," Deacon nodded as his shoulders pushed back. "I pick Saachi."

He'd never imagined that there was a future without Reagan, but the last few days had made it more than obvious that the universe had other plans. And he couldn't waste his life away pining over someone who didn't want him.

"Saachi? You're sure?" Rin questioned, her face wrinkling as she adjusted Deacon's black tie. "I mean, you have the option of leaving single."

"I'm over being alone," Deacon said, head turning to take in the crowd once more. "I'm ready to settle down."

Throughout his twenty six years, he'd sacrificed relationships for love of the game. For a shot at college ball. Then, for the pros. And while the cost had been worth it, now that Deacon had a successful career, he was ready to focus on fulfilling his life in all the ways he'd previously neglected.

"That doesn't mean you should settle," Rin replied, moving the athlete's lapel mic above his silver tie clip.

"I'm not," Deacon argued. "I'm making the choice to make it work with someone."

Rin's lashes lifted as her solemn stare met his. "But what about love?"

Deacon's heart sank. He'd tried to drive down that avenue, and been met with little success. Adult relationships had to be more than love. They required effort.

And he didn't mind fighting to make a relationship work. To make it last.

A little sweat equity always made a final product more valuable in the beholder's eyes. Deacon just didn't want to be the only one putting forth that kind of effort. He wanted to be with someone who was dripping in perspiration right beside him.

And though Deacon hadn't known Saachi long, he could tell she was that kind of person. One who would weather the storm. One who would make sacrifices to be with him. To see him happy.

"Love can grow with time," Deacon said.

"Sometimes it's there from the start," Rin said, her fingers smoothing Deacon's tie before releasing it. "But it's your future, so you get to decide, and I'm sure you'll make the choice that's right for you."

Deacon's brow furrowed at her statement.

Hadn't he told her his selection? What other choice was left to make?

Chapter Thirty-three

A NERVOUS rumble raced through Reagan's body as she awaited Rin's cue from the side of the stage.

This was it.

The moment where she took charge of her destiny. Where she became the sign.

When she played all her cards and put her heart on the line.

There was no more fear of Miller's disproval. No more guilt over sneaking around. No more lies.

No. This time was for the truth.

But how would Deacon respond?

Would he agree to her plan? Or would he send her packing?

"Ladies and gentlemen," Rin called the crowd to attention with her booming voice. "The moment we've all been waiting for has finally arrived. After weeks of wondering which lucky lady would capture Deacon's heart, tonight, we'll have our answer."

Applause erupted and flooded the space.

Rin lifted a single finger as she continued to speak. "But before we get to Deacon's big announcement, we have a special guest I'd like to call to the stage. You haven't met her before, but I think you're going to be a fan." Rin's hand waved Reagan onto the stage. "Put your hands together for Reagan Cassidy."

At the call of her name, Saachi's mouth circled with surprise, and the white in Deacon's eyes doubled. With athletic finesse, he shot to his feet and turned to the side of the stage.

Platform wedges taking the floor, Reagan's fidgeting fingers brushed down the emerald cocktail dress she'd borrowed from Kate. Left bare from the vee neck dress, bright lights warmed her shoulders. As if she weren't already sweating with anxiety.

Reagan glanced to the cheering audience, but their faces were shrouded in a white glow. Still, she could hear their surprised shouts.

"It's the girl from the banquet," a woman called.

A man shouted, "What are you doing here?"

"Go home!" another said.

"Are you joining the show?"

"Get your man, girl."

Reagan's hand lifted in a slight wave of acknowledgement. With the challenge ahead, she needed all the support she could get.

Crossing to center, Reagan paused next to Rin who had risen from her perch. Eyes exuding a reassuring calm, the hostess passed her a handheld microphone.

The flight attendant tried to return a smile, but fretfulness flooded her face when she took in Deacon's tense stare.

"Hello," she said, her alto voice booming over the loud speaker.

His dark eyes bore into her own as Deacon's hand covered his lapel mic. Despite his effort, Reagan's handheld picked up his husky tone. "What are you doing here, Rea?"

"I came to say . . . to say," Reagan's teeth nipped at her lower lip, certain blood was going to pop out of her veins at any moment from her rising blood pressure.

How did Rin perform so coolly in front of this many people? Though she couldn't see them, Reagan knew there were thousands of beady eyes staring in her direction, all wondering the same thing.

What the hell was she doing?

Despite her thrumming pulse urging her to flee, Reagan gulped back her fear and her pride.

She was going to put her heart on the line.

"I came here to say I'm sorry. I'm so, so sorry, Deacon."

A hush fell over the chattering crowd with the exception of a single woman who shouted, "What for?"

"Eh," Reagan replied, a nervous cackle rolling from her chest, "A lot of things, unfortunately."

"Like?" Another audience member prodded her to continue.

"Umm..." Reagan turned to Deacon whose face was still wrinkled with confusion. Both hands gripping the microphone, her lids lifted as she forced herself to hold his critical gaze. "I'm sorry for hurting you. For making you feel confused. You've always been an amazing person, Deacon, and I hate that I made you feel like you were anything less than magnificent. You deserve so much more than that."

"He deserves Saachi," a female voice bellowed.

"Deacon is amazing," another crowd member shouted. A simmer of applause followed the statement.

"I know he deserves someone better than me, and as much as it pains me to admit it, Saachi seems like a good match for him," Reagan tipped her head toward the audience before turning her attention back to Deacon. "But I love you. I *really* love you, and I'm sorry I haven't said it a thousand times before now. I was afraid. Which makes no sense because you're wonderful, and you are the epitome of understanding... well, except for when you punched my brother, but tensions were running high, so I get it. And I don't even care because I love you."

Reagan shifted on her wedges as a surprised hush fell over the crowd.

"But the audience is right. You deserve the best of the best. So if you choose Saachi tonight because she's the right person for you...

I . . . I definitely won't like it, but I will understand. She's been everything I should have been."

Reagan's lips pursed.

Everything she now hoped she could be.

"And . . ." Rin nodded her approval and motioned Reagan to keep going, knowing she came to say more.

Voice growing shaky with nervousness, Reagan continued, "If, however, you look in your heart and find that maybe there's still a piece of you that loves the wrecked person I am, I promise I would spend the rest of my life showing you that I can be the kind of person who is worthy of your love."

Platforms wobbling, Reagan bent to a knee, but realizing the position was unladylike, she quickly pulled both legs under her tea length skirt.

"Deacon, will you marry me?"

A unified gasp sounded from the audience before a hum of voices lifted throughout the theater. Deacon's jaw dropped but no response sounded from his mouth.

Three months ago, Reagan would have had the same reaction if someone told her she'd be on bended knee proposing marriage to Deacon Bailey.

But what she'd once viewed as crazy, now seemed like the most rational move in the world.

Of course, she should settle down with Deacon. He was kind. Reliable. Loveable. He'd stayed the course when she'd tried to push him away.

Deacon was mature. Nothing like her childish father. And she could see that now.

Placing the microphone on the stage, Reagan tugged at the black, silicon ring wrapped around her thumb, but the rubber band wouldn't budge.

"Umm . . . well . . ." she tried to spin the silicon circle, but it held in place, so she held up her hand. "I was going to give you this ring because I thought it was more practical for an athlete, but I guess I won't be doing that now."

Deacon stood before her, his expression composed. Unreadable.

Reagan's gaze lowered as she sat back on her heels, her hand meeting the dip in her dress just above her chest. "Oh, no. You probably think that's a sign, don't you?"

Her scrunched face tilted up toward Deacon's towering frame, soft curls shaking with her dismay.

"What are you saying?" a female audience member shouted. "We can't hear you. What's going on?"

What was going on? Reagan was making a fool of herself in a public spectacle that was likely to go viral as soon as it concluded. If it hadn't already.

"I'm curious as to what's going on as well," Deacon said, hand reaching to his waistband to flip his mic pack to the off position as his forehead creased. "I mean, a proposal? Are you serious?"

The athlete's unusually deep tone and garish volume did nothing to calm her fear of rejection. She'd expected the athlete to be shocked, but she hadn't fathomed an outcome where he was frustrated by her proclamation.

But, of course, he was displeased.

Her confession had meddled in what was supposed to be the kickoff of his new relationship with Saachi.

Reagan squinted as she stared into the bright light drowning out the buzzing crowd.

That's why everyone was gathered in the theater.

They expected to watch Deacon start anew with someone they'd cheered for over previous weeks. Not to watch him sweep away with some unknown stranger.

"Stella convinced me that I could be the sign, but that's not how any of this works is it? I mean, obviously not, because you seem rather upset that I've interrupted your evening." Hands flying to her heated cheeks, Reagan's lashes beat back tears that welled on her lower lids. "I'm sorry. I'm an idiot. This was a terrible mistake."

As she scrambled to push up from the floor, Deacon's swift hand offered assistance. Reagan didn't want to accept the athlete's help, but hoping to keep the last remaining bits of her pride intact, she accepted his aid.

Placing her palm in his for the last time as she rose, she felt as if her heart might burst with sadness. She'd never again know the softness of his touch. The tenderness of his kiss. This was it.

Goodbye.

Meeting his somber stare, Reagan gulped back the flood of emotion rising in her throat. "I'm sorry for everything."

Retreating from the boos resonating about the theater, she attempted to make a hasty turn to exit, but Deacon maintained his steady grip on her hand.

"For *everything?*" Deacon echoed.

His heated glower was hot on her cheeks, but Reagan nodded without meeting his scrutiny. "Except loving you. I'll never be sorry for that."

Deacon's hand let go of hers as his arms folded across his suit. "For the first time in a long time, it seems we agree on something."

"So you don't regret our time together or not together... whatever it was?"

"No. But you were right in what you said earlier," Deacon replied. "What happened here tonight . . . this was a mistake."

Chapter Thirty-four

"I'M sorry. For the embarrassment," Reagan said, her whispered words barely audible over the growing jeers of the audience. "I wish you the best. With Saachi. Or whoever."

Deacon watched auburn curls spill to the sides of Reagan's face as her head sank with defeat. He'd expected the flight attendant to soar off the stage faster than a jet. After all, Reagan was known for running away.

But for the first time, it appeared she was frozen in place. As if her body was so heavy with grief she couldn't move from the very spot where she stood.

Because she loved him.

Loved. Him.

And she'd declared it in front of the world.

Well, maybe not the world, but a crowd this large had to feel the same to a woman as afraid of feelings as Reagan.

When she could have run away. When she could have moved to Chicago and allowed Deacon to fade into history, she stayed.

Lifting her chin with his fingers, Deacon raised Reagan's teary eyes from hiding. "You didn't let me finish."

"I'm not sure there's much more to say," she whimpered.

A gleam radiated from Deacon's dark pupils. "You couldn't be more wrong."

"So we're back to disagreeing?"

"Not entirely," Deacon said, wrapping his arms around her waist as shrieks sounded from the crowd. "I think you're on the right track with some of your thoughts."

A sharp breath escaped Reagan's lips as her body flared at his touch. Her spine went rigid and her mouth parted in such a way that he wanted to delve into its beautiful depths right then and there.

But there were other things to attend to first.

"Love, for example," Deacon went on, pulling her divine warmth closer to his chest. "I find that to be a very agreeable topic, seeing as I love you very much."

Although Saachi was his perfect match on paper, Reagan was the perfect match in his heart, and settling for anything less than her love would never have fulfilled him in the long run. How he ever could have believed differently was almost unreal.

Reagan's sapphire eyes doubled in size as a sparkle of hope glittered in her irises. "You do?"

"You do?" Rin repeated, her brows lifting with excitement.

A sly smile shaped on Deacon's lips. "I do."

"He does what?" someone called from side stage.

He loved her inner fire.

Her stubborn determination.

Her ability to overcome her fears.

"But . . . but . . ." Reagan fumbled with her words as her palms wrapped his biceps. "You said no. You declined my proposal."

"I did," Deacon said. "But only because I wanted to be the one to ask. I've thought of this moment since the first day I met you at Miller's apartment, and hearing you say yes would be my dream come true because I never imagined it possible."

"Yes! She says, yes!" Rin's hands met in a fevered clap as her voice echoed over the speakers.

"Did he propose? He's not even down on one knee." Members of the crowd shouted. "What is she saying yes to?"

"Great question," Rin said, morphing back into hostess mode. "This declaration of love may seem like a surprise to many of you, seeing as you've invested a lot of time and energy into cheering for the two women remaining on the stage. But what you're witnessing here is a love story that began long before this show."

"If they were in love, why did Deacon agree to be a part of the series?" someone shouted.

"Well, you see, Deacon is best friends with Reagan's brother, and that created some complications for them. So Deacon wasn't trying to deceive anyone. He thought he had to move on."

Sliding off her lifted chair, Saachi moved to Rin's side. "It's true. Deacon was upfront about his broken heart from the beginning. He never led me on, so don't hold it against him. I won't be. Everyone deserves happiness."

Deacon flashed Saachi a grateful gaze. She would make a lucky guy very happy someday.

As for him, it was looking like he was going to be happy, too.

Dropping to a knee, Deacon pulled Reagan's hands into his. "Reagan Elizabeth Cassidy, will you marry me?"

Tears streamed down Reagan's reddened cheeks as she flung her arms around Deacon's neck. The force of her body smashing into his, nearly sent the athlete tumbling backwards. Not that he would have minded had she succeeded. Reagan was welcome to topple him to a horizontal any time she pleased.

As her face burrowed into his collar, Deacon pressed a kiss to her forehead, so thankful to be ensconced in her coconut shampoo.

She wasn't perfect, this future wife of his. But she was his. Forever. And that's all that mattered.

"The audience is awaiting your response, love. What do you say?

Do you want to be Mrs. Bailey?"

Pulling back, Reagan's hands ran down his chest, pausing on his lapels. A radiant smiling making her face glow with happiness. "Yes, Deacon. I will marry you."

"Yes!" Rin announced to the crowd, her hands clapping with feverish excitement. "She said, yes!"

Upon hearing Reagan's acceptance, the athlete's forehead melted into hers. "I love you."

"I love you, too," she replied.

"I'm never going to get tired of hearing that," Deacon mumbled, his grin expanding to lengths that made speech difficult.

"Are you going to stare at her all day or are you going to kiss her?" A familiar tenor voice called from the wings. Deacon's eyes flashed up to see Miller standing behind Kate, with his arms circled around her upper body. Loopy smiles beamed across their faces as the crowd began to chant the same demand.

"Our first public kiss," Reagan said, cupping his warm cheeks with her hands. "And it's probably going to be viral by morning."

Head tilting, Deacon's brow quirked as he pulled her body closer. "From hiding to headlines in half an hour. You okay with that?"

"Why not?" Reagan said, brushing his neck with her fingers. "I want everyone in the world to know you're mine."

His lips crashed into hers as his hands wound through silky strands of auburn hair. He claimed her heart and soul in front of an audience of thousands, and Deacon knew then that it had all been worth it.

The hassle.

The heartbreak.

The struggle.

Because it led them to forever.

Epilogue

"**I** CAN'T believe this many people showed up for our engagement party." Reagan curled her arms around Deacon's torso when she finally managed to locate him chatting with fellow Panthers in her brother's kitchen. Wall to wall, the large apartment was packed with friends and family reveling in the couple's excitement. "Miller is probably on the brink of a breakdown with this many people in his personal space."

"He's definitely regretting this show of support," Deacon cackled, wrapping his fiancé's waist. "But it's good for him to open up a bit. Try something new."

"I'm finding I quite enjoy change myself," Reagan said. "Especially this one."

A four carat diamond solitaire glittered under the lights as the flight attendant wiggled her fingers to show off her newest accessory. Deacon had taken the time to find a stone that was ethically sourced, so despite their engagement being three weeks old, the ring was a fresh addition.

"Bling, bling." Rin tugged at Reagan's hand as she approached the happy couple. Her brown eyes assessing the small ice skating rink on her friend's finger. "Your mom was just telling me your ring is incredible, but that doesn't seem to do it justice. What a rock."

Reagan peered at Rin over her lifted hand. "Do you think it's too flashy?"

"There's no such thing as too big of a diamond," Rin replied.

Reagan bumped her hip into Deacon's side. "He did good, huh?"

I'm blinded by the sparkles and your smiles, so I'd say he did better than good," Rin said, her lungs emitting a slight sigh. "If you two weren't my friends, I'd be green with envy."

Reagan squeezed Rin's hand. "If *I* can snag a fiancé, I have no doubt you will, too. And soon."

"Andrew is a fool if he leaves you on the market much longer," Deacon agreed.

"I've actually been thinking about that quite a bit lately," Rin said, fingers streaming through her dark locks, "and I think it's time I also follow Stella's advice and take control of my own destiny."

"What do you mean?" Reagan asked, her back leaning into Deacon's chest.

Rin's hands opened to the couple as her brown eyes sparked with hope. "You proposed to Deacon, and look how that turned out."

Reagan's head lifted to meet her fiancé's loving gaze. "It did turn out rather fabulously, didn't it?"

"I'd say," Deacon agreed, pressing a light kiss to her nose.

"Did you like that she took the lead and proposed to you?" Rin questioned the athlete, her lips pursing in debate. "I mean, I know you ended up asking her, too, so it was sort of a mutual proposal, but did you like that she asked first?"

Deacon looped his long arms around Reagan, his face growing thoughtful. "What man wouldn't want the woman he loves to say she wants to be with him forever?"

"Good point." Rin bit at her lower lip in serious contemplation as clinking sounded throughout the apartment.

Those gathered turned their attention to the evening's host, who was posted in front of the large wall of windows overlooking the city's circle.

"I want to thank everyone for coming out this evening to celebrate Reagan and Deacon," Miller began. "Although it took a minute for the idea of my best friend marrying my little sister to settle in, now, I couldn't imagine it any other way. I can see how you two light up around each other, and I don't know how we all missed it for all those months. Your connection is undeniable, and I couldn't be happier that you found your way together."

"Did we *all* miss it, though?" Kate whispered to Stella who chuckled at the sentiment.

Mrs. Cassidy leaned into the conversation. "I knew Deacon liked her the first time he came to Thanksgiving. You should have seen the loopy smile on his face every time Reagan looked his way."

"Let him have this one," Stella said, looping her arm around Mrs. Cassidy's shoulders. "He needs to think it wasn't that obvious."

"To the happy couple," Miller said, raising his glass in a toast. "Love is the craziest, most unpredictable game any of us play, and while I have no doubt you two are going to cause me to need a few timeouts..." Miller tilted his head toward Deacon, "because she'll always be my little sister, I know that you two make a great team, and this is a match where your victory is a guarantee."

Glasses lifted in reverie before clinking began once again.

"Is there another toast?" Deacon asked, glancing about the room before turning his gaze to Reagan.

She tugged at his pale pink tie. "It means they want us to kiss."

"In public?" Deacon feigned shock as his mouth gaped. "People will see."

"Good," Reagan replied. "Let them watch."

"You're such a Cassidy," Deacon said, nipping at her lips.

"Only for a few more months," Reagan reminded. "Then, I'll be a Bailey."

Wrapping her hands around his neck, she drew him down, her soft lips crashing into his with selfish need.

Deacon's fingers laced through Reagan's silky hair as his hands slid down the curve of her spine. His lips following the line of her curved jaw to the sensitive crook below her ear.

Reagan sucked in a sharp breath. "Deacon. There are people here," she reminded.

With a groan, Deacon practiced restraint and pressed a single kiss to his fiancé's temple. "All this time, I wanted people to see us together, and now I just want us to be alone."

His chest hardened under the weight of her small hands as they swept just above his pecs. "We can't always have our way, Deacon."

"I know," his stole another sweet kiss from her lips. "But sometimes, we can."

ACKNOWLEDGEMENTS

First, and foremost, I have to thank God for blessing me with a creative mind and for the gift of gab, as my mother would say.

To my parents, thank you for your never ending support of my dreams, no matter how lofty they may be.

Next, I want to thank my work girls for allowing me to run a thousand scenarios by them for this story and for being the best beta readers a girl could ask for.

To the girl gang, thank you for being a lighthearted escape when I needed a break.

To my editor, your advice and suggestions are priceless, and I am so appreciative of your support.

And finally, to my husband and son, you are the reason I do all that I do. Thank you for the sacrifices you make as I continue my journey in the writing world.

ABOUT THE AUTHOR

*Tori Kron is a writer, teacher, and mother
who resides in Southern Indiana.
A graduate of Purdue University, she
holds a degree in English Education.
When she's not teaching or writing, Tori can be found
snuggled up with a book, traveling across the globe
with friends and family, or playing with her son, who
has proven to be her greatest adventure yet.*

www.ingramcontent.com/pod-product-compliance
Lightning Source LLC
Chambersburg PA
CBHW020411210626
46816CB00006BB/2231